GIVE 'TIL IT

HURTS

a novel by

MARILYN DONNELLAN

Give 'til it Hurts
By Marilyn Donnellan

This is a work of fiction. Names, characters, places and incidents are the product of the author's imagination or are used fictitiously, and any resemblance to actual persons, living or dead, business establishments, events, or locales is entirely coincidental.

The scanning, uploading and distribution of this book via the Internet or via any other means without the permission of the publisher is illegal and punishable by law.

For all the compassionate people, volunteers and staff, who sacrifice so much to help victims of domestic violence. And to the victims who have the courage to leave their abusers and take the difficult steps forward to safety and new, fulfilling futures.

Prologue

The tangled web of lies, deceit and betrayal cannot be undone until the young executive director of the domestic violence shelter confronts her own mysterious past. And when she is accused of murder, her past threatens to overwhelm her future.

If our charities do not at all pinch or hamper us, I should say they are too small

CS Lewis

When it comes to giving until it hurts, most people have a very low threshold of pain

Anonymous

Chapter One

From Nightmare to Counselor

CJ struggled through the murky darkness, vainly trying to swim against the terror choking the screams frozen in her chest. She strained to understand the angry mutterings circling around her. She could hear her mother's voice but couldn't make out the words. A dark figure stood over her with a broken bottle in his hand. Desperate to save her mother, she thrashed against the chains keeping her in place. She felt herself drowning in her own fear.

Suddenly she sat up in bed, trembling, with sweat pouring off her. The nightmares always ended in the same way: a feeling of suffocation gradually replaced with relief as she realized she was safe in her bed.

Nightmares had been CJ's macabre companion as long as she could remember. She never knew what might trigger them or when, but they were always the same. She tried several times to discuss the nightmares with her mother, Pam, who always dismissed them as caused by something CJ ate. She finally gave up trying to talk to her about it.

As she struggled to awaken from the wisps of nightmare, she heard her mother's shrill voice calling up the stairs.

"Claudette Josephine Pierce!" CJ cringed at the sharp tone of her mother's voice. Whenever her mother used her full name CJ knew she was in trouble – again.

"You left your wet clothes in the washing machine all day yesterday and now I can smell the stink even up here in the kitchen. When are you ever going to learn?"

"Sorry, Mom," CJ yawned as she hollered back. "I'll take care of it in a minute." Groaning, she set up in the middle of the tangled sheets on her bed. Putting her head in her hands, she tried to bring her scrambled brain into some semblance of order. She must have hit the snooze button on her alarm. It was 8:30 am. She had a 9 am appointment with a client at Safe House, the domestic violence shelter where she worked, so she was going to have to hustle to make it in time.

As the dark webs of the nightmare disappeared, CJ stumbled into the tiny upstairs bathroom and splashed some water on her face to help her wake up. Squeezing the last dregs of toothpaste on to her toothbrush, she did a perfunctory swipe of her teeth, rinsed her mouth and then quickly ran a brush through her hair.

"CJ!"

"Coming, Mom!"

She knew from experience she needed to address the laundry situation before she got ready for work. It was better to do what her mother wanted, when she wanted. It was a waste of breath to try and explain to her mother the reasons why the load of clothes was still in the washing machine.

It was 3 am before she got home after spending several hours at the Sumter County Hospital's emergency room trying to convince a battered and bruised forty-year old woman to leave her abusive husband and move into Safe House. CJ had worked full-time as a counselor at the domestic violence shelter since graduating from college.

When she finally fell into bed, laundry wasn't on her mind at all. But CJ knew her mother didn't want to hear about it. She just wanted the laundry done right and done now. Her mother's negative viewpoint on CJ's chosen career was one more thing on her mother's continually expanding list of when-are-you-ever-going-to-learn items. Not since she was a teenager had CJ tried to change her mother's opinion on anything. It was a waste of time, emotions and effort.

For the umpteenth time CJ asked herself if she could afford to get her own apartment. She was twenty-seven years old and still living with her mother in the same house in which she grew up. Something had to change…and soon.

Mom, I love you, CJ silently grumbled to herself as she quickly pulled on a pair of shorts and a tank top and headed down the stairs, through the kitchen and to the laundry room in the basement. But it is times like these I can almost understand why my father left you. Your constant negativity really gets to me some days.

Because of her mom's attitude, CJ could never seem to get up the courage to press her mother with hard questions about why her father left or the reasons for the divorce.

Maybe I'm afraid of the answers I'll hear. And I know exactly what Sadie would say if I told her maybe my nightmares are somehow tied to my father.

Sadie, the executive director of Safe House, had appointed herself as a mentor for CJ. Periodically she would prod CJ to talk about her feelings, but CJ couldn't bring herself to talk about herself. She didn't like the possibility of changing the way she thought Sadie viewed her: from a giving, compassionate and hard-working employee to just another one of the many domestic violence victims she saw every day.

She'd probably tell me my nightmares mean my father was abusive…My mother and I are victims…I'm repressing memories…I'm suffering from post-traumatic syndrome…and on and on. Piffle! I just don't have time to deal with all this. Besides it doesn't matter now, I'm an adult and don't need to dredge up all that stuff.

"Piffle" was the only word CJ used when she felt like swearing. Her Christian upbringing put brakes on using anything stronger. She used the word whenever she was frustrated, which seemed to be more and more frequently.

Last night she caught herself saying "piffle" a couple of times as she became increasingly frustrated trying to convince Susan to leave her abusive husband. Susan looked puzzled the first time she heard the word, but once she understood it was CJ's attempt at swearing, she smiled for the first time that evening. It was extremely difficult for battered women to find something about which to smile, so it was a good moment for both.

Every time CJ talked to a woman struggling with domestic violence issues, vivid memories of the day of the murder of her best friend Trina's mother eleven years ago lurked at the back of her mind.

The year of the murder, Trina and CJ were finishing their junior year in high school. They lived a block away from each other so they always walked to school together. The night before the murder, CJ tried calling Trina, but she hadn't answered the phone. CJ hoped she was okay as she walked toward Trina's house that fateful morning.

Trina's house always seemed to be frowning. The front porch sagged, the window curtains were never open and the wood siding needed paint. Cracks in the sidewalk and driveway were speckled with sprouts of spring pushing up beside the dried weeds of last fall.

CJ knew better than to ring the doorbell, since Trina's stepfather worked the night shift and was usually trying to sleep when Trina was leaving for school. She shuddered as she remembered the one time she mistakenly rang the doorbell. She would never forget the horrible yelling and cursing Jack was directing toward Trina when she jerked open the door.

Not wanting to repeat the episode, CJ gently knocked on the door. Trina had obviously been waiting for her. As she stepped out the door, quietly closing it behind her, CJ could tell by the expression on her face there was something wrong. The sunny day suddenly darkened with clouds of apprehension.

"What's the matter, Trina?" CJ asked in alarm.

Trying to hold back tears, Trina responded as she walked down the sidewalk beside CJ, "I came home from school yesterday and found Mom on the floor crying. She had a black eye and she was holding her arm like it hurt really bad. I had to take her to the emergency room. It's a good thing I got my driver's permit last week or I would have had to call an ambulance."

CJ abruptly stopped walking, turned and looked at Trina in shock.

"Oh, my God! Is she okay? What happened?"

"Jack beat her up again. She has a cast on her broken arm and one eye is swollen shut, but she'll be okay," she said with silent tears dripping off her chin. CJ put her arm around Trina and gave her a hug.

"I wondered why you didn't answer your phone last night. Why didn't you call me?" CJ asked, resuming her walk with Trina. "I would have come over and gone to the emergency room with you."

"I was so upset and focused on trying to help Mom I didn't even think to call you. I thought about it after we got home, but I didn't want to wake your mom."

CJ began to lengthen her stride and pick up the pace as she became more and more agitated at what Trina was telling her.

"Hey, slow down, CJ!" Trina hollered as she looked up from her contemplation and realized CJ was speeding up.

"Oh, sorry," CJ said. Her long legs and Trina's short legs weren't always compatible when it came to walking. Trina was just barely five-feet tall, with porcelain skin, vibrant, curly red hair and curves in all the right places. CJ was almost six-foot tall, lanky and with dark skin and black hair from her Cherokee Indian heritage. The girls had learned to ignore the incessant teasing from their classmates about the contrast in their looks.

Slowing her steps, CJ tried to match Trina's lethargic walk. She knew they would probably be late for school at the rate they were walking but she decided she didn't care; it was more important to find out what happened and comfort her best friend.

"While we waited to see the doctor," Trina said angrily through her tears, "I begged her again to leave my step-dad and go to the shelter. But just like she said to me dozens of times after he hit her (her voice changing to a whiney falsetto as she imitated her mom) 'It's okay, honey. . . Your step-father didn't mean it...He loves me...It's my own fault he hit me...I should have put the mail in the right spot on the table. . . I knew he was drunk...I should have stayed out of his way,' and on and on and on...it just makes me sick!"

She stopped in the middle of the sidewalk, her whole-body trembling as she began to cry in earnest. CJ hugged her again and then pulled Trina down to sit beside her on a conveniently placed tree stump.

"She wouldn't even let me call the police. She told the doctor she fell down the stairs... and we don't even have stairs," Trina wailed.

"I don't get it," CJ said angrily as she jumped up and stomped her foot in frustration, "Why won't she leave him?"

Before Trina could reply, CJ continued her tirade.

"I can't for the life of me see what she sees in him. She should never have married him. And you better stay out of his way. You've been lucky so far he hasn't come after you."

"I know, CJ. If he ever does come after me, I'm calling the police."

Trina paused for a moment in contemplation, gulping down her sobs and wiping her tears away with a tissue she pulled from her pocket.

"I guess when my dad was killed in an accident at the factory ten years ago Mom was lonely and couldn't resist the first man who came along. Jack worked with my Dad and he just kind of took over after the accident.

"Mom called the police one time after he broke her nose but he got all apologetic, brought her flowers and everything, so she dropped the charges."

"It's just not right," CJ protested furiously, clenching her fists in anger. "I don't understand why God allows this kind of thing to happen. I can't stand to hear the way Jack treats your mom. Neither one of you should have to go through this."

"Thanks, CJ. You don't know how good it is to have someone to talk to about this."

Then Trina shook herself, furiously wiped another track of tears from her face and stood up, straightening her shoulders in determination. "Let's go. We're going to be late for school."

There seemed to be nothing more to say, so CJ tried to calm down and walk quietly beside Trina; both in somber moods while they finished walking the ten blocks to school.

Although she didn't say it to Trina, CJ believed it was stupid to stay with someone who beats you up, even though the pastor at her church frequently talked about how divorce was a sin. Her own father hadn't been around since she was four years old. That was twelve years ago. CJ was pretty sure he had beaten her mom. Her frequent nightmares were probably related to her father.

Her mom refused to talk about her father. CJ couldn't remember what he looked like and didn't even have a picture of him. Her mom said after the divorce she destroyed every picture with him in it. CJ sometimes wondered what he was like and where he was. They had no other family members. Her mom was an only child and both of her grandparents passed away before CJ was born.

After seeing what is happening with Trina's step-father, maybe I'm better off not having a father in life, she angrily thought to herself as she walked up the school steps with Trina, just in time for the final bell.

The girls joined into the rhythm and routine of school; a welcome distraction from Trina's problems at home. Still, CJ's mind wandered and worried instead of focusing on her classes. It was so frustrating to not be able to do anything to change Trina's situation.

After band practice the girls decided to stop by Trina's house for a snack before their trip to the library to study for a chemistry exam and to check out college catalogues online. Trina assured CJ her step-dad wouldn't be at the house.

"Jack is always gone for several days after he beats up my mom," Trina said with a shrug.

They had by agreement moved away from the depressing topic of Trina's step-father. They were giggling about the cute new boy at school as they burst through the back door into the kitchen. The girls froze in horror at the sight of Trina's mother lying on the floor in a pool of blood, her blank eyes seeming to stare in bewilderment at the ceiling.

The stark terror and agony in the screams exploding from Trina were something CJ knew she would never forget. A kitchen butcher knife stuck out of Trina's mother's bloody chest and her face was swollen and black and blue from an obviously brutal beating. The arm in the cast lay twisted in a terrible parody of a goodbye wave.

CJ stood rooted to the floor, unable to move, her body and mind frozen in fear and shock. Trina collapsed to her knees at her mother's side, ignoring the pools of blood. There was blood spattered all around the kitchen; the floor was slippery from it and the metallic smell of blood was gagging.

"Mom! Mom! Don't leave me!" Trina screamed as she shook her mother's shoulders. Her voice sounding like the agonizing wails of a small child in terrible pain, Trina began to cry and moan. In an act of final desperation, she reached out a trembling hand to pull the knife from her mother's chest.

"Don't touch it," CJ screamed as she rushed over and pushed away Trina's now bloody hand.

"Come on, Trina. You can't help her now. We have to call the police." Gently, CJ raised Trina to her feet. Trina sagged against her, sobbing uncontrollably, her clothes covered in her mother's blood. CJ helped her to a chair at the kitchen table.

"Stay right here, Trina," she begged, tears streaming down her own face. "I'm calling the police."

Her senses reeling from the sights and smell in the tiny kitchen, CJ somehow managed to swallow her own screams and nausea and reach for the phone hanging on the kitchen wall, her hands trembling as she tried to punch in the 911 call. Later she could not recall exactly what she said to the operator. She could only remember saying repeatedly, "Oh, God. Oh, God."

It seemed to take forever before she heard the sirens and the squeal of tires as the police car braked to a stop outside the house. She could see through the living room window the flashes of red and blue from the lights of a police car. She moved Trina to the living room where they sat on the worn couch, out of sight of the grotesque body. Trina seemed to be frozen in shock, her eyes glazed and her skin whiter than CJ had ever seen it.

She left Trina sitting on the couch and shakily opened the door for the two policemen who entered the house with their guns drawn. Her mind and body seemed to operate on automatic pilot as she sat down beside Trina while the police carefully moved into the kitchen. When they were sure there was no one else in the house, they called for their forensic investigative unit and started asking the girls questions. CJ held Trina's trembling, cold hands while she answered the questions of the police. Trina was in a daze, unable to respond to the questions. It wasn't until hours later, long after the police had removed the body and Trina was safely at her grandmother's house, her own reaction set in.

For two days CJ couldn't seem to stop trembling and crying when she was alone in her bedroom. Trina never knew.

She has enough to deal with, CJ convinced herself, making sure she stayed as calm and supportive as she could whenever she saw Trina.

CJ's mother's only comment after CJ explained the reason for the blood on her clothes and hands was: "It's terrible but Trina's mom is better off now. Her sorrows are over. Mine never end." Stung at her reaction, CJ decided not to tell her mother about her own struggles trying to deal with the murder. If she had told her she knew what her mother would say, "You think you have problems…" and then go off on a litany of her own woes.

Trina was devastated by her mother's death. CJ helped Trina and her grandmother plan the funeral, since there was no other family around. Pastor Bert Neely of the Faith Community Church where Trina and her grandmother attended was a great help; walking them through the legal process of dealing with a death and officiating at the funeral. CJ couldn't believe all the red tape involved and the constant barrage of questions by the police and the media.

The police were confident Jack was the murderer. His fingerprints were all over the knife.

The fingerprints and his history of beating his wife were enough for them to put out an all points bulletin for him. But unable to find Jack, the case went cold.

The summer after the murder – just before their senior year in high school – terrified Jack would return and kill her too, Trina moved in with an aunt in California and tried to make a new life for herself. CJ heard from her on birthdays and Christmas, but it was the extent of their contact. She knew Trina couldn't help but associate her with the horrible murder of her mother, but it still hurt to no longer have the close relationship with Trina.

The last year of high school passed in a fog for CJ. Getting up in the morning and making it through the requirements of each day without Trina took a strength which seemed to fade by evening. Later, she couldn't remember how she managed to keep her grades up.

While the kids around her talked about boys, college and their futures, CJ could focus on anything but the murder. A constant swirl of what-if questions and self-recriminations haunted her mind, like the broken film of a movie endlessly playing the same scene over and over again.

Why didn't I take more seriously what Trina was going through? CJ asked herself a thousand times. I should have been able to help get her mom to the shelter. I should have said something to the counselor at school that day. If only we'd gone directly to the library instead of going to the house first; maybe someone else would have found the body instead of us. Why did God allow such a terrible thing to happen?

She would then inwardly scold herself for wishing such horror on anyone else and for not having more faith in God. During the last conversation Trina had with CJ before she moved, she thanked CJ for her support. Then she said:

"You have been an incredible friend and I couldn't have gone through the whole thing without you. You were so calm. You have a real gift for helping people in crisis."

CJ's mental and emotional struggles related to the murder, the daily irritations of her mom and the academic requirements of her senior year in high school pushed Trina's words into the back of her mind. It wasn't until her first year in college, when she was trying to decide what would be her major, Trina's words wandered back into her awareness.

A counselor in high school had arranged for her to do volunteer work at Safe House as a way to cope with the stress of dealing with the murder and to learn more about domestic violence. The counselor knew Sadie, the executive director, who could help CJ through the necessary paper work and criminal background check so she could volunteer. Two or three times a week after school or on the weekends, CJ would help with the housekeeping duties at the shelter or just play games with the temporary residents' children.

Her conversations with Safe House staff about their chosen careers helped her to begin to heal emotionally and to understand more about domestic violence and why so many women stayed with their batterer. Soon after CJ started volunteering at the shelter, a young woman with eyes black and blue, almost swollen shut from a beating, returned to her husband the next day after her arrival. She had shown up at the shelter in a police car with her terrified one-year-old child in tow at the same time CJ was leaving for the day. Angry and frustrated, CJ stomped into Sadie's office, so upset she could hardly talk.

"Why would she go back to him?" CJ asked, her voice shaking and tears threatening to spill from her eyes. "She could be killed!"

"CJ, remember it was her decision to make," Sadie said gently. "We can't make her stay at the shelter, even though we wish we could. All we can do is to keep our doors open for her because she'll be back, probably several times before she has the courage to leave him."

"But why?" CJ persisted. "It just doesn't make sense."

Sadie came out from behind her desk and put her arm around CJ. "Let's sit and talk about this," she said, guiding CJ to a worn sofa. "A woman who is abused has been so beaten down emotionally by the batterer's words she believes it is her fault when he hits her; and he doesn't hesitate to tell her it is her fault either," she continued.

"Most batterers were themselves a part of a family where the father abused the mother. Often the women saw their mothers being abused, too, so neither the batterer nor the woman knows of any other way to handle anger except through violence. Our job is to help these women understand what is happening and try to show them they don't have to put up with it. And sometimes, although it is rare, the batterer is the woman. In those cases, the man is usually so embarrassed he won't get the help he needs either.

"We provide anger management classes for the batterer, but few take advantage of them. Victims of domestic violence have usually been abused for so long, it is like a form of brainwashing. The abuser is good at isolating the victim, so she has no money, no job skills and little to no sense of self-worth. As a result, the woman sees no way out. What is known to her – the abuse – seems safer than the unknown and being on her own without job, money or home, especially if she has children."

CJ took a deep breath and ask the question rolling around in her head since the murder. "Sadie why would God allow these terrible things to happen to women?"

"You are asking the same question Job asked centuries ago. Do you remember his story in the Bible?" Sadie reached over to her desk and picked up a well-worn Bible. "Satan challenged God and said the only reason Job worshiped Him was because everything was going well for him. So, God allowed Satan to afflict Job. He lost all his children when they were killed in a freak accident. His wealth was taken away from him and he became physically ill with boils all over his body."

"Oh, yeah, I remember the story from summer church camp. God never did answer the question 'why' Job asked. He simply told Job to have faith in Him."

"Very good, CJ. Rarely will we know why bad things happen. But as our faith is strengthened we learn to trust God regardless of what happens, knowing we are in His hands and He will give us the strength to cope.

"But, let me caution you. Women who are going through the horrors of domestic violence do not want to hear Christian platitudes. They need love and acceptance. Too many Christians are so adamant about divorce being a sin, they would rather a woman stay in a violent situation than leave her husband."

Sadie stood up. In a rare display of agitation, she began to pace the floor as she talked. "Do you remember Judy? I was here last year when she came to the shelter. She told me her pastor said if her husband was beating her it was undoubtedly her fault because she had not learned how to be properly submissive to her husband. And, if she just got herself right with God her husband would stop beating her."

Tears filled Sadie's eyes as she stopped her pacing and sat back down on the sofa beside CJ.

"Judy was killed by her husband after she left the shelter and went back to him. He was convicted of murder and will spend the rest of his life in prison. Now her three young children have no mother and no father. I refuse to believe my loving God wants a woman to stay in an abusive relationship. I strongly believe she needs to get herself and her children into a safe situation and pray God will change her husband's heart. If the husband refuses to get help, she needs to get on with her life; and if staying safe includes divorce, she should do it."

CJ sat quietly on the sofa trying to absorb what Sadie told her. What she said made sense. Listening to the passion and commitment in Sadie's voice, she realized for the first time what an emotional toll dealing with battered women could have on a person.

Sadie stood up and took down a plaque from the wall behind CJ. As she handed it to CJ she said, "CJ, one of the most important things you can do to help these women is to take care of yourself: emotionally, spiritually and physically. If you are not up to your best in every way, the pressure and stress will get to you very quickly as you deal with these hurting women and children. In fact, very few staff in this business stays on the job for more than two or three years. The stress can be too much to handle for many people.

"The words on this plaque have been a daily encouragement to me since we opened the shelter ten years ago. I firmly believe loving these hurting women and their children is the most important thing we can do. Why don't you read the plaque out loud to me?"

CJ noticed the plaque hanging on the wall, but really hadn't paid much attention. Now she focused on the meaning of the words as she read:

"*Love always protects, always trusts, always hopes, and always perseveres.*

Love never fails." I Corinthians 13:7-8

Sadie gently held CJ's hand and said, "CJ, I know you are a Christian and a very loving person. You obviously care very deeply for these women. But if you are going to make helping others your life's work, you need to know it does not come without a price. Giving of yourself will hurt; sometimes it will hurt so much you won't know if you can keep on doing it. And you won't always understand why God allows such things to happen.

"But this type of work also comes with tremendous rewards: seeing women who finally find the courage to leave abusive relationships, literally saving their own lives and the lives of their children."

Sadie handed the plaque to CJ and said, "This is now yours. I want you to keep it as a reminder of why and how we do this job."

As CJ went home that afternoon, she considered Sadie's wise words. She hung the plaque on the wall in her bedroom, looking at it every time she was tempted to quit working at the shelter, or when the frustration levels and emotional pain seemed to be more than she could bear. Sometimes even spending time reading the Bible and praying didn't seem to answer her questions, but it always gave her a calmness she knew could only come from God.

Her time at the shelter helped her better understood what had happened to Trina's mom and why. Understanding soon blossomed into a passion for helping the women to break the cycle of violence. Within a year, because of her volunteer work at the shelter and remembering Trina's words, CJ to begin to think seriously about the possibility of a career in social work. Maybe helping domestic violence victims was what God wanted her to do with her life.

Her good grades resulted in some small scholarships to help pay for college. With some student loans and, beginning in her freshman year in college, a small stipend from Safe House, she could cover the costs of undergraduate and graduate degrees at the University of Chicago.

She knew she never would have made it through those difficult years if it hadn't been for the support, prayers and encouragement Sadie gave to her. When CJ completed her undergraduate degree, Sadie approached her about working full-time for the shelter. It was a no-brainier for CJ. She had found a way to help women and children in crisis; a tangible way to prevent them from continuing to be victims: victims like Trina and her mother.

Despite the way her childhood nightmares expanded to include Trina's Mom, CJ never wanted to forget the horror and helplessness of that day. The memories of the murder always strengthened her personal resolve when a battered woman resisted moving into the shelter.

CJ's present musings about the past ended abruptly when she reached for the basement light's string and took the last step into the dark, musty basement to take care of her load of wash.

"Ouch!" she hollered as she hit her head on one of the low wooden beams holding up the sagging kitchen floor above her. CJ lost track of how many times she bumped her head on the same beam. She seemed to be always thinking about something other than the location of the inconvenient beam when she entered the basement. She would love to saw a big gouge in the beam right where she always hit her head.

Just my luck the house would fall down if I attacked the beam, she grumbled to herself as she rubbed her forehead.

The house was forty-years old and in desperate need of repairs, as evidenced by the dank smell in the basement, the sagging kitchen floor and the peeling blue paint on the outside.

The only good things about the house were its location and the fact she could pay a smaller amount to her mother for rent than she would have to pay for an apartment. The property on which the house sat was probably worth more than the house itself. It was located a short drive north from Chicago and only ten miles from Lake Michigan. In the past few years most of the houses surrounding theirs had been totally renovated or torn down. Trina's house was one of the first to be torn down.

New, modern houses lined the narrow tree-lined streets. Their little house sat like a rusty, broken and abandoned toy in the middle of the shiny new homes on the outskirts of the Village of Fredricks. At least the people in the neighborhood were friendly and she felt safe when she took her infrequent walks through the nearby park. If she could convince her mother to sell the house and move into a nice apartment maybe she wouldn't feel so guilty about moving out herself.

"Back to the task at hand," she said out loud. CJ opened the squeaky lid of the old washing machine and wrinkled her nose in disgust. It was July and the humidity felt like it was at least ninety-five per cent. The closed-in basement was ripe with the smells of mold and mildew.

Whew! I guess I'll have to wash this load again, CJ sighed. Adding a bit more soap than usual and some bleach to hopefully get rid of the sour smell permeating her clothes, CJ turned the knob to start. The washing machine clanked and groaned but thankfully came through for her and started the wash cycle so she trudged back up the stairs into the kitchen.

"I told you the clothes would stink if you left them in the washer," Pam said, her thin lips set in a tight line of disapproval. She was standing in front of the microwave heating up a frozen breakfast sandwich. She was still in her bathrobe and had obviously not yet combed her hair, her frizzy gray hair sticking out in spikes. Pam was sixty years old, but she looked like she was eighty: her face lined with wrinkles making her face look like aged parchment. CJ figured she must have gotten her height from her father since her mother was only a little over five feet tall.

"You were right, Mom," CJ said apologetically, through gritted teeth. "I'm washing the load again. Could you please do me a favor and put the load in the dryer when the washer stops? I'm going to be really late for work if I don't get a move on."

"That place doesn't pay you enough for what you do for them. When are you going to get a better job somewhere else, or at least ask Sadie for a raise? You need to get a place of your own."

It was the first time her mother had suggested she get an apartment. Knowing she didn't have time to discuss the issue in detail, CJ simply responded, "I'll talk to Sadie today, okay?"

"Don't forget. And yes, I'll take care of the load of wash for you but don't expect me to go up and down those stairs more than once today. You know how much pain I'm in."

Pam was on Social Security Disability for a back injury, a result of lifting a heavy patient five years ago at the nursing home where she worked. CJ's rent money didn't make a huge dent in the costs of maintaining the house, but she knew it helped reduce some of the financial pressure on her mother.

It seemed to CJ if her mom could just find something to fill her time during the day maybe she would feel better and wouldn't be so negative all the time. Her never ending litany of aches and pains made CJ welcome the stress and long hours of her job, just so she wouldn't have to listen to her mom's complaints.

Negative thoughts about her mother always made her feel guilty, undoubtedly an unreasonable carry-over from her years of absorbing guilt and hell-fire-and-brimstone teaching at the little church down the street. She remembered a lot of contrasting Sunday school lessons when she was growing up about "love one another." But the sermons and lessons on sinning always seemed to leap out of her memory and grab her more frequently than did the ones on love.

CJ stopped attending church every week when she was in college. She seldom went to church anymore. Too tired and too busy, she mentally excused herself; one more checkmark on her sub-conscious list of daily sins. Maybe all her hours at the shelter would balance out the good-bad list of her life. Besides, she hadn't yet reconciled in her mind how God could allow such terrible things she saw every day at the shelter to happen to innocent and vulnerable women and children. She still believed in God, but she was beginning to think He really didn't care about what happened to people.

Her mother attended church twice on Sunday and went to prayer service on Wednesday night. CJ was still waiting for the "love one another" teaching of the church to catch hold in her mother's attitude. She was sure her mother's constant negativity contributed to her own complacency toward spiritual things.

Here I go again. I'm getting as bad as my mother at criticism. Mom's life is Mom's life. So, suck it up, CJ, and get ready for work!

It was a good thing she loved her job so much. Giving of her time and energy to help women was so rewarding emotionally. She was frustrated frequently by women who repeatedly went back to their abusive husbands or boyfriends, but otherwise, she was happy at the shelter. The feeling of accomplishment was incredible when a woman and her children managed to escape the abuse. Those accomplishments kept her committed to her job.

CJ liked the fact she didn't have to dress up in a suit and high heels every day for work; she'd never been one for the frilly girly stuff. Anyway, a counselor wearing business attire was too intimidating to women who came to the shelter with only the clothes on their back, and usually trailed by several wide-eyed children.

But her chosen career had not come without a price: a stack of student loans and living with her mother in the cramped two-bedroom house. The tiny salary she got at the shelter probably meant she would be paying on the loans until God was in a wheelchair, she often thought facetiously. Given the rates of crime and domestic violence in and around Chicago, her master's degree in social work pretty much guaranteed she could find work anywhere, but the degree seemed to have little positive impact on how much she was paid. It had taken her several years to get the graduate degree, since she had to work full time and go to school part-time. But at least she had not added to her school debit.

As she ran up the stairs to her bedroom, CJ's mind swirled with the decisions she knew she was going to need to make in the very near future. She took a quick shower and pulled on a denim skirt and a bright, colorful sleeveless blouse. While she pondered the best way to approach Sadie about a raise, she cinched tight the wide belt she added to her outfit and mentally enumerated her wish list for the day.

Okay, God, CJ philosophized, while you are at it, besides getting me the raise, an apartment and maybe a cute boyfriend, why don't you take care of my nightmares? Then my life would be just about perfect!

CJ considered it ironic, although she believed God didn't really care about the daily happenings of people, she continued to shoot small arrow prayers heaven-ward when she wanted or needed something. I guess it is just a habit, she mused.

First college and then her job had left her little time for a boyfriend. She experienced the predictable, awkward groping of boys during her infrequent dates in high school and was disgusted by the whole thing. She was too busy working and going to college to have time for dates. Even so, she still sometimes fantasized about an ethereal Prince Charming.

Shrugging off the fantasy musings, CJ slipped on a pair of loafers, pulled her hair into a pony tail, and touched her lips with a little lipstick before heading downstairs.

"Bye, Mom," she yelled over the sound of the television in the living room. Neither expecting nor waiting for a reply, she bounded down the chipped concrete steps outside the front door and slid into the aging car sitting in the driveway.

Uttering another one of her many unconscious prayers each day she put the key into the ignition. Please God, let the car start. With a bang and chug, the rattle-trap car's engine turned over and lurched into gear.

Fortunately, she didn't have far to drive; she could even walk if the car broke down, as it seemed to do frequently. Safe House, located just two miles from CJ's house, was hidden in the trees at the end of a dirt road near the forest preserve. To protect the shelter residents from raging husbands and boyfriends, the location of the shelter was known only to the staff, the police, and to the few carefully screened board members and other volunteers.

Although the women signed confidentiality agreements when they came to the shelter, past and present residents rarely needed to be reminded how important it was to not tell anyone where they were staying.

In the twenty years since the shelter opened, the staff knew of only one time a resident made the mistake of telling where she was staying. The battered twenty-two-year-old girl missed her mother and when asked she told her mother not only was she at Safe House but where it was located. When the girl's boyfriend threatened to kill the terrified mother, she blurted out the location of the shelter. The girl was murdered; shot by the enraged boyfriend when she stepped outside of the shelter to have a smoke.

Over the years the story of the girl's death passed from resident to resident, helping to guarantee the secrecy of the location. Even the media cooperated in keeping the location of the shelter confidential.

Chapter Two

The Future Brightens

As CJ approached the shelter she rehearsed in her mind the conversation she wanted to have with Sadie about her salary. The administrative offices for Safe House were located on the second floor of First Bank, just off Maple Avenue. She would have to meet Sadie at the office after she took care of some counseling appointments at Safe House.

She parked the car behind the shelter and walked up the gravel path to the nondescript three-bedroom house. Although it looked rather small from the outside, there was room in the house for at least eighteen people to stay overnight. Located thirty-four miles north of Chicago, Safe House was a refuge for women from the inner city as well as for women in Sumter County. Today it was bursting at the seams with seven women and eleven children, ranging in age from six months to twelve years old.

"Hi, Julie," CJ warmly greeted the matronly house mother taking a batch of chocolate chip cookies out of the oven. The aroma of the cookies seemed to permeate the walls of the large yellow kitchen, encouraging visitors and residents to linger and share tidbits of their lives.

"You look a bit worn out, CJ," Julie replied with an understanding smile. "You did good work last night."

"Thanks. Sorry I'm late. How is Susan doing?"

"She's terrified, but she's already talking about going back to her husband. I convinced her to wait until you got here before she made her decision. She's in the blue bedroom with her son."

CJ grabbed a warm cookie, dodging Julie's playful hand slap, and then headed for the blue room. She stopped, turned around and through a mouthful of cookie she asked Julie if she knew where Sadie was.

"Oh, she's at the office. Should be there all day. Did you need to see her?"

"Yeah. If she calls in would you let me know so I can talk to her?"

"Sure. I'll let her know."

The morning was a blur of one-on-one counseling with Susan and two other frightened and bedraggled women struggling with decisions which could literally save their lives. This was a good day since the women all decided to stay another day at the shelter and to file restraining orders against their spouses. CJ learned early in her work at the shelter, battered women were always more than just physically beaten. The constant emotional abuse wore away any positive sense of self-worth and feelings of self-confidence.

Every effort was made to get the women and their children out of the shelter and into alternative housing within three days of their arrival. Safe House was an emergency shelter for women in the middle of a domestic crisis and was not a long-term residency.

Each one of the bedrooms was crowded with three sets of bunk beds, a battered dresser or two, the floors usually cluttered with toys. A talented and creative volunteer had painted each room differently, including fantasy scenes running cheerfully up the walls and on to the ceiling. The blue room was a vision of an English garden, while the green and pink rooms danced with unicorns, fat cheerful dragons and butterflies. The large living room was decorated by another volunteer in soft earth tones using a country theme. Comfy sofas and chairs meandered around the room, while pictures of laughing children and cozy homes paraded around the walls.

Just before noon, Julie hollered to say Sadie was on the phone. Excusing herself from a rare, light-hearted, and noisy game with three of the children, CJ walked rapidly to the reception area and picked up the phone.

"Hi, Sadie," CJ said rather breathlessly. "I know you are busy but do you think you could fit me into your schedule this afternoon? I have something I need to discuss with you."

"Oh, that sounds ominous," Sadie laughed. "Sure. How about four o'clock?"

"Great. I'll be there."

As always, time seemed to fly by when she was at the shelter. She suddenly realized she had only fifteen minutes before she had to be at Sadie's office. On a good day, with little traffic, it would take her ten minutes to drive from the shelter to the office. She would have to hustle if she didn't want to be late. Sharon, the other counselor at the shelter, agreed to fill in for her for the rest of the day since CJ wasn't sure how long she would be at the office with Sadie.

As she drove through the small village of Fredricks she was amazed again at how much her hometown had grown in the last couple of years. New homes and office buildings popped up like rabbits. There was more traffic than usual on the narrow streets leading the way to the picturesque town square downtown. Still, she made it to the bank, and the Safe House office, just in time for her appointment. Sadie moved the administrative offices away from Safe House last year as the demands for more space for women and children took precedence. The old two-story bank sat on the northwest corner of the town square. The Safe House second-floor office looked out over the town square. A gazebo and the statue of one of the town's founding fathers flanked an ancient oak tree in the center of the square. A labyrinth of flowers blazed trails to each monument to the town's history.

Rehearsing in her mind what she would say to Sadie, CJ parked the car behind the bank and walked up the stairs at the back and down the hall through the potpourri of little used offices. Her heart was pounding as she rapped on the door of Sadie's tiny office.

"How are you?" Sadie asked with enthusiasm as she opened the door and gave CJ a warm hug, motioning her to a tattered chair in front of her desk.

Glancing at her mentor as she sat down, CJ thought Sadie looked a bit more worn than usual. Sadie was close to retirement age and her years as the founding executive director of the nonprofit clearly aged her; especially in the last five years. When CJ first met her ten years ago, Sadie's hair was brunette; now it was completely gray. She couldn't help but wonder if the constant, daily struggle to handle the administration of the agency was taking its toll on Sadie. Normally a bit matronly in appearance, Sadie looked thinner. She was about 5'5" tall but seemed to be a bit more stooped over than usual. For a fleeting moment, CJ wondered if Sadie was ill.

Now CJ was even more apprehensive about asking her for a raise. Finding funding for the shelter was always difficult. But now with the traditional and major funders like county and state governments tightening their financial belts, it was tough to meet the annual budget. She didn't know exactly what Sadie was getting paid, but it couldn't be much. Now here she was planning to add to Sadie's stress by asking for a raise.

"Actually, Sadie, I'm a bit nervous," CJ said, picking at a loose thread on the ancient chair.

Sadie leaned back in her rickety desk chair, cocked her head and asked with a smile, "Whatever for? You know you can talk to me about anything."

"I know, but this is different." Taking a deep breath, CJ jumped right into the topic of salary.

"Sadie, I know how tight the budget is for Safe House, but I really need to know if there is any chance of a raise; maybe within the next year?"

"Is that what is making you so nervous? My goodness; I've been so busy I've neglected to talk with you about this issue, haven't I? I'm sorry. I've been meaning to bring up a related topic for the past couple of months."

"Bring up what?"

"CJ, how would you like to be my associate director?" She paused, her brow furrowed in concentration, while CJ sat frozen in stunned silence.

"You're young, but you certainly have the education, experience and skills we need at Safe House. I think you'd be great in the position and I think you are ready for it. What do you think?"

CJ didn't know what to say. This was not what she had expected from her conversation with Sadie, but she could feel a kernel of excitement take root and begin to grow as she thought about the possibilities of such a position.

When CJ didn't respond, Sadie kept talking. "Initially, you would spend about half of your time with me learning the administrative side of things, staffing some of the board-level committees, and doing some public relations stuff; the other half of your time would continue to be spent counseling. I want to gradually faze you out of the counseling half and hire someone else to fill your current spot, and then you'll be able to focus all of your time on community education and administration issues."

Ideas and possibilities flashed like lightning through her awareness as CJ continued to sit in silence. The counseling job was frustrating sometimes. She would spend long hours counseling a woman living in a violent relationship, only to have her meekly go right back into the terrible situation. When it happened, often CJ felt like a mouse on a treadmill, making no headway but constantly moving. This new position would undoubtedly provide her with opportunities to educate women on how to avoid relationships which might lead to abuse and to get her off of the frustration treadmill.

CJ mentally shook herself from the ideas swirling in her mind; time for that later. Sadie broke the lengthening silence by saying, "Oh, and by the way the position comes with a significant raise. The position has been vacant for almost two years, so there is money already in the budget for it. Well? Yes, or No? Or do you need time to think about it?"

"No...I mean...yes. I'll take the job!" CJ blurted.

For the next hour CJ and Sadie reviewed the job description and finalized the necessary paperwork for her change in position and salary. Tired, but ecstatic, CJ stood and shook hands with Sadie.

"Oh, come on," Sadie bubbled, "I think this deserves a hug, not just a handshake," grabbing CJ to give her another hug, her smile lighting up the room. Everyone who met Sadie for the first time was struck by her smile; it had become her trademark because it was always so genuine and spontaneous; never forced.

"I'm thrilled you are willing to take on this added responsibility. It won't be easy. But I know you'll do a fantastic job."

CJ turned and shakily headed for the door, but Sadie stopped her with a hand on her arm and a sheepish grin on her face.

"I think I would be remiss if I didn't tell you I have a rather selfish motive for offering you the associate director job. I'm planning on retiring in the next couple of years. When I do retire I want to be able to recommend to the board of directors you be hired for my position; if you agree of course, and providing you prove yourself in the associate position. But I don't want you to say anything to anybody about this possibility until the board has had the chance to see you in action and not until I announce my retirement."

CJ dazedly walked back to the chair and plopped down in shock. It was unthinkable Sadie would leave Safe House. It was even more incredible Sadie believed she could take over as executive director.

"Are you okay, CJ?"

"I am speechless!"

"That's a first," Sadie laughed, "But does it mean you'll consider it?"

"Absolutely! But are you sure you have to retire?"

"Yes, it's time. I am finding I just don't have enough energy any more for the job. It's time I let a young, talented and compassionate professional – namely you – step in."

With tears of gratitude in her eyes, CJ finally said her thanks and goodbye to Sadie.

All the way home, her thoughts and emotions boomeranged from: "I can finally get my own apartment and maybe a new car!" to "How can Safe House survive without Sadie?"

At the board meeting next week, Sadie would announce she hired CJ for the associate director position. It would be the first board meeting CJ attended. There had been no need for her to attend before. The mysterious workings of the board had always been Sadie's purview. She knew from past conversations with Sadie, dealing with the board members was sometimes difficult, but she said their support and leadership were critical to the success of the shelter. Board members provided a wealth of experience in a variety of administrative areas as well as opening doors to corporations and high net worth individuals for contributions.

As she pulled up into the driveway at home, it suddenly hit CJ she was going to have to get some different clothes. Casual dress wouldn't cut it if she was going to try and make a good impression on board members. CJ jumped out of the car and raced up the front steps.

"Mom, I have great news!" CJ hollered as she burst through the door, spotting her mother in her customary spot on the couch watching television.

Not waiting for her mother to say anything, she plunged into the telling. Her mother's eyes widened in disbelief and then, for the first time in a long time, CJ saw a smile tug at the corners of her mother's mouth. Maybe God answered wish lists after all!

Chapter Three

Reality Sets In

George Maniaci was pontificating – again.

"I remember when Safe House had a reputation for having the best programs in the state of Illinois," he stated emphatically from his chair at the end of the board room conference table. "For twenty-seven years Sadie Neely always made sure women got the help they needed and there was enough money to run the agency. Now we can't seem to get the funding we need and I'm not confident the programs are adequate to the needs. I think it is...."

CJ found herself fidgeting and starting to tune him out so she slipped on her poker face and forced herself to pay attention. She waited for him to take a breath so she could maybe ease him back on track. She desperately wanted him to attack the agenda items instead of rehashing his complaints. The retired city manager was a member of the Safe House volunteer board of directors and he was the chair of the programs committee; the committee meeting where CJ sat uneasily. CJ was frustrated George seemed to be wasting so much time on unnecessary comments about the past instead of moving forward on the critical items on the committee's agenda.

While she agreed the agency was struggling for adequate funding, it was nothing new. And, she knew women who came to the shelter always received all the help they needed. It rankled he seemed to be inferring they didn't or intimating the lack of funding was her fault.

"I didn't see you at the last fundraising event," CJ silently scolded George. He seemed to do little to help other than show up at meetings and complain. Sadie reminded her last week, even with all his faults George was a valuable resource since he seemed to know everyone in Sumter County.

"Calm down, CJ," she said to herself with an inward sigh. "Get him back on track."

Leaning forward in her chair ready to diplomatically pounce into the one-sided discussion, CJ tried to reasonably evaluate George's litany of complaints. Her frustration stemmed from board members like George spending more time complaining than helping her to identify solutions. Attendance at board and committee meetings was down. She suspected a lot of the board members used her youth and lack of administrative experience as excuses to reduce their volunteer involvement with the shelter.

"No way am I going to let them think I'm intimidated or I'm shaking in my boots." She didn't want anyone on the twenty-member board or on the committees to know how inadequate she sometimes felt, and how much she wished Sadie was here in her place. When George paused for a breath, CJ spoke up, carefully choosing her words.

"I agree. Sadie's years of leadership of this organization were incredible. No one will ever be able to replace her. What do you think we need to do with our programs to build on her legacy? What are some ideas we can recommend to the resource development committee to increase our funding?"

With her words, George seemed to forget what he'd planned to say next and got the committee back on the agenda. With a grateful but silent sigh, CJ jotted down the appropriate notes as the meeting lumbered toward its conclusion. As she said goodbye and "thank you for coming" to the committee members trailing out of the bank's conference room – which Safe House was allowed to use free of charge – CJ decided she ought to go by Sadie's home for a quick visit and to update her on the board meeting. She was mentally and emotionally exhausted from the meeting. But, if Sadie was feeling well enough to talk, she could use some advice on how to keep George on track in the meetings.

Bert, Sadie's husband, answered the phone when she called and asked if it would be okay to come by.

"Sure," Bert responded. "Sadie is always better after a visit from you."

"How is she doing today?"

"She has good moments and bad moments. Right now, she's sleeping," he said. "We'll talk more about it when you get here. Okay? Oh, and be careful driving on our street. It hasn't been plowed yet and the snow is pretty deep."

"Okay. I'll be careful. I should be there in about fifteen minutes."

Sadie retired last year, earlier than she expected, after it was discovered she had breast cancer. She finished her second round of chemotherapy when the doctor gave her the bad news: she had maybe six months to live. When Sadie calmly told her the news four months ago, CJ was devastated, although – when she thought about later - not really surprised.

Over the previous few weeks she noticed Sadie was looking much older. She had an almost skeletal look from the excess of weight loss, a major change from her previously pleasingly-plump appearance. The loss of her hair and the gray pallor to her skin, glaring signs of the horrendous toll of the chemotherapy and the insidious takeover of the terrible disease; signs CJ tried unsuccessfully to ignore.

CJ gladly stepped in as interim director when Sadie first became ill and then retired last year. At the last meeting, the board finally crystallized their requirements for the new executive director. At Sadie's urging, CJ put in her application for the position. Some days – like today - she wasn't sure it had been a good idea to apply. Sadie's constant advice and encouragement were the only things keeping her from resigning as interim director.

But, Sadie was more than her encouraging mentor. Sadie was a good friend and CJ couldn't imagine life without her. In many ways Sadie had been more of a mother to her than her own.

At the thought of losing Sadie, tears of grief and frustration filled CJ's eyes as she turned the car down Wildwood Avenue, a few blocks away from Sadie's home, the icy snow cracking beneath the tires. She pulled off to the side of the street when she found a spot without snowdrifts, giving herself time to calm down and dry her tears before she drove up to the house. As she tried to compose herself, shivering in the cold despite the blasts of warm air from the car's heater, CJ considered the past year.

When she accepted Sadie's offer to be associate director, neither of them had any idea how quickly CJ would have to try and step into Sadie's shoes. The board agreed with Sadie's suggestion to have CJ as interim director while the board started the search process for a new executive director. CJ was taking classes in business management at the local community college to fill in her gaps in knowledge.

In the first few months in her new position, CJ was frequently terrified she would screw up the agency so much it might never recover. Then she would have a talk with Sadie. Or, she would stop by Safe House and talk to a woman who was determined to get out of her abusive relationship and to make a new life for herself and her children. She always left such conversations buoyed with hope and with renewed determination to fulfill Sadie's vision – and now her own - for the shelter.

During the past year, dealing with the myriad of daily administrative and program tasks had not been nearly as difficult as learning how to work with the board members. She was discovering board members usually had unstated and shadowy reasons for joining the board. And, each board member seemed to play a distinctive role during board and committee meetings. CJ came up with her own descriptive names for each one of them. Names she shared only with Sadie to try and bring some humor with her on the visits.

George was The Ancient One. He was always trying to bring up the past instead of focusing on the future. CJ suspected his board membership was more about trying to re-live the glory days of his power as a city official than it was about helping Safe House.

Christine was The Blocker. Christine was single and a successful marketing executive. Twenty years ago, she pulled herself out of an abusive situation, with the help of Safe House staff. She appeared to have some issues related to men and showed it by the way she tried to block just about every recommendation made by the male board members. CJ did not doubt Christine's commitment to the agency, but cooperation was not one of her strengths.

Bob the Nitpicker was a certified public accountant and an incredible resource for CJ on financial issues related to the shelter, her studies for her social work degree did not include anything on financial management. But he and Christine constantly butted heads in and out of board meetings. It didn't seem to matter what was the issue or proposal addressed by the board, Bob had a long list of detailed recommendations he discussed with CJ after every board meeting. It never failed. Christine would call a couple of days after the meeting with her own recommendations for CJ.

Her comments were always preceded by: "Has Bob called you yet? If he has, just ignore what he says. This is what you need to do…"

CJ thought both needed to get a life. They spent way too much time thinking and talking about the minutest detail related to Safe House.

Julie brought homemade cookies to every board meeting. The other members usually disregarded her timid suggestions, so CJ nicknamed her The Mouse. She had come to realize, however, despite Julie's unassuming and shy demeanor, she had a very sharp mind. If CJ was having difficulty sorting out her responses to a controversial board issue, she would meet later one-on-one with Julie to get her reasonable and always helpful input.

And on and on it went. Each of the board members contributed a lot to her ability to get things done, especially when it came to positive community relations and fundraising. But adapting to the idiosyncrasies of the individual board members was a herculean task. The first time she staffed a board meeting without Sadie present was one of the scariest and most confusing meetings of her life. How much was she supposed to talk? Did she have the right to disagree with a recalcitrant board member or to voice her opinion on a policy the board was considering?

The next day after the first board meeting, CJ went to Sumter County Hospital to see Sadie who was recovering from a double mastectomy. She greeted Sadie with a kiss and asked her how she was feeling.

"I'm doing fine, now you are here," Sadie said with a weak smile.

CJ dropped herself dejectedly into a chair next to Sadie's hospital bed. "How in the world did you do this for so long? I'm ready to kill myself or strangle some board members."

Sadie smiled and reached out to put her hand on CJ's arm. "Don't let them get to you, CJ. Just remember, the individual board members have the potential to be a tremendous resource for you. Each of them was chosen for the board because of a specific ability or experience from which you and Safe House can benefit." She paused for an obviously painful breath.

"You just have to be sure you stand your ground on administrative and program issues which are your responsibility. Get the board members to focus on strategic, long-range planning and on policy setting: everything else is your job. Don't let them take over your job. Besides, you can outwait them, since the board members have term limits and will eventually leave the board."

Silent for a moment, CJ sat up straighter then looked at Sadie with a grin as she said, "I've decided board members are best compared to mutant ninja turtles; they seem to be torn between sticking their heads inside their shells or fighting like ninjas."

Sadie let out a subdued hoot of laughter. "Best description I have ever heard!"

Just then, Bert, Sadie's husband walked into the room, greeting CJ with a smile and a hug before he leaned over the bed and gave Sadie a kiss. He gently squeezed her arm, asking her how she was doing. CJ could tell by the way he greeted Sadie, he still adored her, even though they had been married for almost forty years. With an ache in her heart for what the two of them must be going through, she stood up and attempted to leave.

"Where are you going? You don't need to leave on my account. I just stepped across the hall to visit a parishioner. I think you should stay," looking at Sadie for a confirmation nod. "I know Sadie looks forward to your visits."

Bert was the senior pastor at the Faith Community Church and helped Trina and CJ plan the funeral after Trina's mother was murdered. He was always Sadie's biggest supporter from the time she broached the idea of starting the shelter. The couple had two sons: Christopher, an attorney with a law firm in Chicago, and Brent, a youth minister at a tiny church in Wauconda. CJ didn't remember much else about them since Chris had been two years ahead of her in high school and Brent was two years behind her. All she remembered about them was their height; both over six feet tall. In high school, she always noticed boys taller than she was.

But then the murder of Trina's mother had crowded all thoughts of boys from her head. Brent had been at the house a few times when CJ came to visit Sadie, but she had not seen Christopher since high school. Sadie frequently talked proudly about her boys, so CJ felt like she knew them vicariously. CJ stayed a few more minutes at the hospital, trading humorous stories of the antics of the board members, and then she headed back to the office. The talk with Sadie helped and at the next meeting she could be less introspective on how she felt board members viewed her.

After the second meeting of the board she started making the mental list of humorous and descriptive names for the individual board members. It helped her to cope and to focus on what was important. Besides, Sadie enjoyed her descriptions and outlandish stories about the board members.

Now, an incredibly difficult year later, CJ sat shivering in her car, down the street from Sadie's home, trying to get control of her emotions while wrestling with whether to withdraw her executive director application; and what impact such a decision would have on Sadie. Her mind in turmoil, it suddenly hit her. The best way she could honor Sadie's legacy with Safe House would be to stick it out and make the shelter even better – should the board decide to hire her.

With a new resolve and an arrow prayer heavenward for strength, CJ carefully negotiated the car through the snow and up the street to Sadie's home. She greeted Bert with a hug when he opened the door.

"How is she?"

"Not good, CJ."

There was a deep sadness in Bert's eyes and he appeared to have aged considerably since Sadie was diagnosed with terminal cancer.

"What can I do?"

"Thanks for asking and thank you for coming. I think the best thing you can do for her is to talk to her about Safe House the way you always do. Your visits mean so much to her."

Squaring her shoulders, she walked into the living room to sit next to the hospital bed set up for Sadie when she could no longer walk upstairs. Softly she said, "Hi, Sadie."

At the sound of CJ's voice, Sadie slowly opened her eyes and smiled her glorious smile. Greeting Sadie with a gentle kiss, she proceeded to entertain her with the day's antics of the board members. CJ could tell Sadie was very weak, but she bravely carried on the predominately one-sided conversation. When Sadie's eyes fluttered, like she was trying to stay awake, CJ knew it was time to leave and let her rest.

It was the last time she saw Sadie alive. That night, on January 17th, Sadie died. Bert called her at six in the morning to let her know. Struggling with her tears, CJ thanked Bert for calling and asked if she could do anything to help with the arrangements.

"Thank you, CJ," he choked through his tears, "But Sadie made sure all the arrangements were completed several weeks ago. She didn't want me to have to worry about it."

Trying vainly to come up with profound words of comfort, CJ simply said, "I'll miss her. And my thoughts and prayers are with you."

After she hung up the telephone, she gave in to the grief and sorrow tearing across her like the waves of a raging sea. But, by 9 o'clock, CJ had dried her tears, was dressed and on her way to Safe House to let the rest of the staff know about Sadie's death. Her voice raw with emotion, she called every board member to let them know. She then put together a press release about Sadie's legacy and her death.

Three days later, Bert tearfully but joyfully gave the eulogy at the service celebrating Sadie's life. The church was packed for the service. Politicians, business executives, peers of Sadie's profession, and hundreds of ordinary people jammed into the pews; each person's presence a tribute to the impact of this one woman's life. Three women of different ages and lifestyles shared humorous and poignant stories of how their lives had been forever changed because Sadie had the vision and fortitude to establish the Safe House shelter for victims of domestic violence. By the time they finished their stories there was not a dry eye in the place.

As CJ sat in the service, she silently strengthened her resolve to honor Sadie's memory by doing everything she could to make Safe House even better and to educate the community on the issues of domestic violence. There was a moment during the service when she realized how far away from God she had gotten. If she wanted to emulate Sadie, she ought to really get closer to God. But the fleeting thought was not strong enough to overshadow the myriad of problems associated with being the shelter director.

Not many of the attendees at the service chose to face the five degrees below zero temperatures to attend the brief burial service at the cemetery; temperatures made even worse by the frequent, wild gusts of chilly wind. At the end of the service, CJ walked up and dropped a single, red rose on to the top of the flower-laden casket. It felt like her tears froze on her face as she shivered and turned to walk back to her car.

"Claudette Pierce?"

She turned around and looked up into brilliant blue eyes set in a vaguely familiar face.

"Yes, I'm CJ," surprised someone would call her by her given name. Only her mother had called her "Claudette" since her sophomore year in high school.

"Hi, I'm Chris Neely, Sadie's oldest son."

"Of course! It's been so long since I've seen you. I didn't recognize you. I'm so sorry about your mother. I loved her dearly. She was a fantastic woman. I'm so glad I had a chance to know her. I will miss her so much."

Suddenly stopping what to her ears sounded like babbling, she waited for his response. As she waited she couldn't help but notice the chiseled jaw and wavy dark hair. It was obvious he worked out. Even bundled up against the cold he looked terrific.

"Thank you, CJ. She was a very special person. We are all going to miss her," he said, obviously having difficulty speaking because of the tears choking his voice and threatening to fall from his incredible blue eyes. "I am just glad to know she is now free of her suffering and rejoicing in the presence of Jesus."

Nodding sympathetically, CJ started to shiver from the cold.

"Do you mind if we walk toward my car as we talk? I'm freezing to death."

"Certainly, I'm sorry. I guess my mind isn't functioning too well," he said with a crooked smile.

CJ turned and started walking toward her car. Chris walked beside her, their boots causing the icy snow crust to crunch with a snap-crackle-pop as they carefully made their way toward the cars. When she inevitably slipped on the ice, Chris grabbed her by the arm to keep her from falling. His firm grasp on her arm warmed CJ in more ways than one. It was the first time she had felt such a heat from the touch of a man. It was a surprising and wonderful feeling.

"Look, we're having a small gathering of friends and family at the house. My mom and dad talked about you all the time. It would mean a lot to all of us if you would join us. Can you come?"

"Sure…I'd like that," she managed to say with a blush. I never blush. So where did that come from?

Chris nodded and then opened the car door for her. As she sat down in the driver's seat, she tried to remember the last time a handsome man opened a car door for her. It was a very pleasant experience, despite the cemetery setting.

"I'll see you at the house," he said with a smile. He closed the car door, turned and walked away.

Smiling to herself, she started the car and carefully eased it into gear, her tires spinning briefly before grabbing hold on the ice. The late model red Volvo was her first major purchase after Sadie hired her as the associate director at the shelter. The heavy car was a dream to drive in the snow

Pulling out of the cemetery on to the county road, CJ decided before she went to Sadie's house she would make a quick stop at her mother's apartment to see how she was doing. She had no idea the funeral would be the last time she would see Chris for more than four years. And the reason she would see him would be for something totally different than romance.

Chapter Four

Harassment

CJ loved her apartment. Until the harassment started a month ago, she felt safe and happy in the little nest she built for herself. Now she was uneasy, and it made her increasingly angry. The heavy breathing on the telephone and the disgusting, hateful notes she often found under the windshield wipers of her car were horrible intrusions into her peaceful home.

She worked hard to make her apartment a haven for herself in the four years since Sadie died. And now it was threatened by some maniac's obsessions. She carefully selected a potpourri of antique furniture and knick-knacks which seemed to whisper her name when she found them in the dusky corners of the quaint antique shops around Chicago. Antiquing had become a relaxing and delightful break from the pressures of her job as executive director of Safe House. When she was poking around shops she could forget for a while the seemingly endless line of battered and broken women and children who glided through the shelter like horror-stricken ghosts.

CJ was surprised how much she loved feminine, frilly décor; not something she would have imagined when she was younger. She painted the walls of her tiny living room a cheerful yellow, a perfect backdrop for the colorful watercolors and oils of flowers she painted herself; usually in the wee hours of the morning when she couldn't sleep after a nightmare. An antique wing chair sat at an angle in front of the living room window and was covered in a yellow English garden print. Next to the chair was a round end table, draped in pale blue chintz and topped with an antique glass lamp with a white, frilly shade. The cherry wood drop-leaf table backed up to the compact kitchen was just big enough for two matching chairs; the seats covered in the same fabric as the wing chair. CJ loved the way the wood from the table and chairs seemed to glow from the years of careful dusting done by the 84-year old woman from whom she had purchased the set.

Under her large painting of roses on the wall opposite the wing-backed chair sat a puffy two-cushion love seat, upholstered in a crisp yellow and blue stripe. The infrequent visitors could catch glimpses of her bedroom through the hallway off of her living room in which sat a queen-size, four-poster bed haphazardly piled with lace-covered pillows sitting on top of a delicate white embroidered coverlet. Gauzy white chiffon gracefully draped the windows and swayed between the four posts of the bed. The bedroom walls, she painted sky-blue. Antique pictures of elegant ladies framed in a variety of well-polished woods paraded around the walls. Bookshelves, painted white, tucked into every available nook and cranny of the apartment, and were filled with the classics, mysteries and science fiction books, most read several times by CJ. Even the little kitchen featured antiques: old appliances and utensils sitting proudly on shelves above white cupboards.

The whole antique thing had started when she and her mom worked together to pack up their belonging in the old house after it sold. CJ was taking things out of the attic when she found a trunk buried behind the Christmas decorations. Surprised at her find, her curiosity peaked, she dusted off the top and carefully opened the trunk. Inside was a beautiful, hand-made quilt. Although slightly faded, the patches of the quilt made a breathtaking flower garden of color. CJ carefully held the quilt in her arms as she backed down the rickety attic stairs.

"What do you have there?" her mom asked as CJ walked into the living room where she was taking pictures down from the wall. CJ held up the quilt, and her mother's eyes widened in disbelief.

"Oh, my goodness. I forgot all about your great-grandmother's quilt," she said as she reached for it.

After admiring it, CJ's mom said she wasn't interested in keeping the quilt and gave it to her. It was the beginning of CJ's interest in antiques. Her great-grandmother, Sonja Pierce, made the quilt while she was a young woman waiting for her husband to return from an expedition to the Pacific

Northwest in the mid-1800's. After finding the quilt, CJ had a lot of fun doing some research on the Pierce family history and decided then and there she wanted to surround herself with the comfort and warmth of old things.

Until the harassment started she hadn't felt alone or insecure in her apartment since she was surrounded by the loving symbols of the lives of relatives and mysterious people who had lived long before her. She framed the quilt in a Plexiglas box and it hung on the wall above her bed. She knew it was a bit big for the apartment, but she loved it so much she didn't care. The lively patterns and colors in the quilt became the inspiration for many of her paintings.

"I have had enough!" CJ yelled as she sat up in her rumpled bed and slammed down the receiver on the white antique phone after the disgusted breathing of some twit filled the earpiece for the third time in a week. The call had awakened her from an unusually sound sleep. It wasn't often she slept in and to have this jerk wake her up was too much. She took the day off from Safe House after working twenty-four hours without sleep.

It was 3 a. m. before she had fallen into bed. One of the counselors had gotten sick and CJ was filling in for her until she was better. She quickly got dressed, not even thinking much about what she put on. After a perfunctory swipe of a toothbrush and a brief brushing of her long hair, CJ grabbed her coat and purse, and headed for the door.

She stopped her headlong rush out the door long enough to make a scrawling note on a piece of paper, stuck it inside a folder sitting on the table - which she tucked under her arm - and then angrily stomped down the stairs to her car. Squealing the car tires as she left the apartment parking lot, she tromped on the gas as she entered the street and headed for the police station.

The new police station was several miles away, so there was enough time for CJ to get more and more pissed off at whoever was harassing her. When she had to slam on the brakes to avoid a bicyclist who crossed in front of her without looking, she sat in the car for a few seconds trying to calm her racing heart and to get herself under control. A sudden honk behind her startled her into driving the car a bit more sedately to the police station. As she approached the new two-story brick building housing the police administrative offices and a small jail for overnight prisoners, her mind whirled with questions about who could be harassing her and why.

CJ knew the police chief well. Chief Jason Johnson or his deputies were frequent visitors to the shelter. It was easier and safer sometimes for the residents if the police came to the shelter when a woman decided to file a complaint against her batterer. There had been occasions when the batterer had tried to intimidate the victim as she entered the police station with a Safe House counselor: a stupid idea, but CJ had found batterers weren't always the brightest bulbs on the planet. Chief Johnson was a good financial supporter of Safe House and CJ had been thinking about asking him if he was interested in serving on the board of directors; she just hadn't gotten around to it yet.

She parked in the newly paved parking lot and walked into the police station, still permeated by the smell of new construction. CJ hardly noticed the leaves of the elm and oak trees surrounding the building, reversing their green coats to fashionable shades of gold, orange and red for the coming fall. After successfully navigating the familiar but tiring security gauntlet, CJ walked into the main area where several police officers with whom she had worked greeted her. Waving her hand distractedly at their greetings, she walked down the hall and stuck her head into an office.

She knew the Chief was out of town at a conference and decided Sergeant Richard Rakowski was her best bet for prompt action. The Sergeant had been a big help to her last year when one of the shelter clients had killed her boyfriend in self-defense. CJ nicknamed him "Teddy," since he resembled a big cuddly polar bear with his beard and mane of white hair and his roly-poly physique.

"How ya doin, CJ?" The Sergeant looked up at her with a wide grin and leaned back in his chair, his considerable paunch hanging over his belt. He was getting close to retirement and had decided to be a desk jockey while he finished out his tenure. He had a comfortable grandpa look to him, but CJ had been told by Chief Johnson he had been a formidable street cop in his heyday.

"I'm upset, Sergeant. Can I talk to you for a minute?"

"Sure. What's on your mind?"

"I'm being harassed, and I am tired of it. My patience has run out!"

"What!" His chair thumped to the floor as he sat up in surprise. "When did this start and why haven't you come to me before?"

"Well, it started about a month ago. A few heavy breathing telephone calls and some disgusting notes on my car. And I didn't come to you before because I figured it would go away. I believed it was some idiot who had somehow found out who I was and was upset because Safe House was helping his wife or girlfriend."

CJ slammed her folder down on his desk.

"Inside are all the notes I have received and the dates and times of the calls I have gotten so far. Now, what can you do about it? I am getting fed up with this twit and I want it to stop."

Sergeant Rakowski carefully thumbed through the notes.

"Have you touched these?"

"Of course, I've touched them," CJ said with sarcasm. "I picked them up, read them and then stuck them in the folder."

"Hey, don't get snippy with me, missy."

Sergeant Rakowski leaned toward her and frowned, his snapping blue eyes showing shades of the cop he had been. "I just wanted to know if anyone besides you had touched them so we can check for fingerprints. Okay?"

CJ took a deep breath and plopped into the old leather chair sitting in front of his messy desk. "I'm sorry, Sergeant. It's not your fault. I am just fed up with this whole thing."

"Understood. But not a good idea to take your frustration out on me. Okay? Now, don't worry about it, CJ. Let's see what we can do to help."

Lumbering up from his desk Sergeant Rakowski's uniformed five-foot-eight stocky frame seemed to fill the tiny office as he stepped around CJ and stuck his head out the door.

"Sam!" he yelled. "Get your sorry butt over here."

The Sergeant sat back in his chair. "I have just the person to help you out with this: Detective Sam Harris. He's a rookie detective up from Chicago and he claims to be a specialist in harassment."

CJ stood up as the detective entered the room: all six-foot five of him. She silently gulped as she looked up into the most incredibly beautiful grey eyes she had ever seen. His wavy blond hair and tanned skin gave him a California surfer look.

"Sam, this is CJ Pierce. She's the director of Safe House, the domestic violence shelter, and she's got a harassment problem. Why don't you put your fancy college education to work and see if you can help her? Take her over to the small conference room and get the info you need.

CJ could not get her voice box to work, so she said nothing, simply nodded and followed Sam out of the office. My oh my, she thought to herself, I'll follow you anywhere.

"I'll get us some coffee and then we can talk," Sam said over his shoulder. "What do you take in your coffee?"

"Just cream, thank you." CJ was pleased her voice box seemed to be working again.

The conference room was bare, except for the oblong table and a few chairs. The city had obviously decided pictures and decorations to be frivolous wastes of taxpayer money. Sam walked into the room with their coffees and the interview started without preamble. He had an easy, affable manner about him. He took a few notes on a small pad as CJ talked and he then looked at the information in the folder.

"I'll see if we can get any finger prints off these and then I'd like to put a tap on your phone. Are your fingerprints on file, Ms. Pierce, or do we need to get a set of them for comparison purposes?"

"Call me CJ. And my prints are on file from a case Sergeant Rakowski helped me with last year."

"I'd like to go to your apartment and plant a listening device on your phone. When would be a good time?"

"How about around four this afternoon?"

"Great! I'll see you then."

CJ left the police station in a bit of a daze. It was another stressful day at the shelter, with two new women to admit to the shelter, but she managed to make it back to her apartment by four, still thinking about Sam's incredible gray eyes.

Sam showed up with all kinds of technical gear. He looked around the bright living room, smiling that beautiful smile of his.

"Nice." He said. "Very homey. My apartment looks like a bomb went off in it, which is why I don't spend much time there."

She watched as he attached her land line to some type of recording device.

"What do I do if the harasser calls me on my cell phone?"

"Has he called you on your cell phone?"

"No. In fact I don't know how he was able to get my home number since it is unlisted."

"Nowadays it's easy for anyone. All you need is a computer and you can get just about anyone's information. If he calls you on your cell phone hit your recall button and see if you can get a phone number and then let me know.

"Here's my cell phone number," he said, handing her a business card. "Do you have a business card I can have?"

"Sure. Give me a minute and I'll get it for you."

She left Sam in the living room while she walked down the hall to her bedroom where she kept her purse. It took her a couple of minutes to dig out her business card. When she walked back into the living room she was surprised to find Sam standing over her reading lamp, his hand just coming out from under the shade as though he had turned the light off. For a moment, she was puzzled as to why he would be turning her light off since she didn't remember turning it on, but his astonishing smile as he turned toward her caused the incident to fly right out of her head.

He shook hands with her and started toward the front door. She had just started to close the door behind him, when she saw him turn around.

Lazily, but without a hint of hesitation, Sam looked into her eyes and said, "By the way, gorgeous, how about having dinner with me tonight?"

"I can't tonight, Sam, but how about Saturday night?

"Terrific! I'll pick you up at seven," he said with an incredible, self-assured grin.

That was how her whirlwind romance with Sam started. For the first time CJ knew what people meant when they talked about love at first sight. It was strange, though, as she was dressing to go out with Sam on their first date, there was a moment when she thought about Chris Neely, Sadie's son, wondering why he had never called her after they met at the graveside service. Mentally shrugging her shoulders at the vagaries of men she finished getting ready.

Dating was not something she did often. Her job kept her so busy and she had not met anyone in the small town who interested her, other than Chris.

She peeked out her window and saw Sam drive into the parking lot; right on time. The 1972 red Corvette Stingray fit her first impressions of Sam; a bit of a playboy and a daredevil. Smoothing her hair and taking one last look at herself in the full-length mirror, she tried to calm her nervous stomach as she waited for him to ring the doorbell.

"Wow!" he said as she opened the door. "You look great."

"You don't look so bad yourself," CJ returned with a grin. Sam was wearing a pair of khakis, a crisp white shirt open at the neck and a navy-blue blazer, setting off his tan beautifully.

CJ felt like she was floating as she took his arm and walked down the steps of her apartment wearing her favorite red dress, topped with a white, antique lace shawl. She liked the fact she could wear high heels and not tower over Sam like she did with most men. On the drive to the restaurant she found herself relaxing and enjoying their conversation. He asked her about her job and she asked him why he had become a detective. The thirty-minute drive to the quaint little Italian Restaurant in downtown Chicago went by too fast. But they lingered over dinner and the easy conversation continued. She felt like she had known Sam longer than just for one day. She was surprised to find it was after midnight before they were forced by the restaurant's closing to head back to Fredricks.

"I have a confession to make," he said as he walked her to her apartment. "I have had my eye on you for a while. I saw you at the fundraiser the police fraternity had for Safe House but couldn't get close enough to introduce myself. You were surrounded by high mucky-mucks and I didn't want to bother you. So, when you showed up at the police station I knew it was my lucky day."

CJ was flattered but something about his comment bothered her. "How did you know the Sergeant would ask you to help me?"

Sam brushed off her question with a laugh and said, "Oh, I just knew."

CJ let it go, deciding it was no big deal.

"I'll pick you up at 9 a. m. tomorrow, so we can go for a hike," he said after he kissed her goodbye at her apartment door. She was glad he hadn't tried to come in. It was one bit of awkwardness she didn't need. After she closed the door, she wandered into the bedroom and dreamily sat down on the edge of the bed and thought about the evening. She realized she felt a little uncomfortable when he assumed she would agree to the hike, but she quickly shoved the discomfort away, chalking it up to his style.

It was the beginning of CJ's first serious relationship, she ruminated to herself one day after a romantic cruise with Sam on Lake Michigan. Sam was attentive, planning all sorts of fun and interesting dates fitting into both of their busy schedules. It felt good to have someone else in charge of a part of her life. Everyone at the shelter always looked to her for direction and decisions, so Sam's take-charge attitude was a nice relief from the daily stress.

Although Sam wanted to take the relationship to the next level, CJ made it clear to him she just wasn't ready to have sex with him. Several times she started to ask him if he was a Christian, but she always managed to shove the question into the deep recesses of her mind. She was confident she would automatically know if he was not a believer. Within a few weeks of their first date, Sam and CJ eloped to Las Vegas.

Chapter Five

From Happiness to Horror

She had never been happier than she was when she got on the plane at the O'Hare Airport with Sam and headed for Las Vegas. As Sam dozed beside her, CJ looked out the window, but her eyes weren't seeing the clouds or the baby-blue sky: her vision was sparkling with the rosy future she anticipated. She realized they really didn't know each other well, but she figured the story books were right about love at first sight. We'll figure it out as we go, she sighed contentedly and then closed her eyes to continue the dreams of their future.

They didn't even tell their families or co-workers they decided to elope. They figured they could tell everyone when they got back to Fredricks. As far as everyone knew, they were on vacation somewhere. They decided to elope rather than have the expense of a wedding since neither she nor her Mom had much in the way of financial resources for an elaborate wedding. Besides, Sam and CJ knew so many people in Fredricks there was no way they would be able to have a wedding without offending someone they might forget to invite.

They got married at a horrible, tacky, little wedding chapel on the Strip. The overweight Elvis impersonator who performed their wedding ceremony made them both giggle. They finally broke into gales of laughter as they ran out of the wedding chapel. With so many conventions in town, the only hotel room they could find was a bit off the beaten path. It was a three story older motel; clean but a bit on the well-worn side. They grabbed a late dinner at the Denny's around the corner and then played some slot machines in the hotel lobby until after 2 a. m.

"Let's go to our room, honey," Sam said after he'd won $50 on the third machine he played. "It's time we got better acquainted."

At his words, CJ could sense a tingle of anticipation or fear – she wasn't sure which – in the pit of her stomach. Sam decided to take a shower and CJ put on the new ridiculously tiny white negligee he bought for her before they left Fredricks. The nightgown wasn't anything like the old comfortable t-shirt she usually wore to bed, but she didn't object since she really wanted to please him.

Never mind the motel is tacky, she said to herself as she sat on the gauche heart-shaped bed waiting for Sam to come out of the bathroom. The important thing is I'm here with Sam and I'm a married woman.

The longer she waited for Sam, the harder her heart pounded and the more nervous she became.

She couldn't figure out what made her heart race so much. Sam had pushed her hard to have sex before their marriage but her church background – at least that's what she thought was causing her hesitation – made her push him away every time he got too close. She liked it when he kissed her, and she liked kissing him back. But every time he wanted more she would make excuses: she was having her period; she had a headache; or she had to go to work the next day. She could tell he was getting frustrated and exasperated with her. She finally told him she was a thirty-three year old virgin. He thought it was funny, his harsh laugher and a crude comment showing a side of him she had not seen before. She chalked it up to his embarrassment and his way of dealing with her hang-ups.

Now, here she was waiting to find out what she had missed while all her peers were shacking up. She was Mrs. Sam Harris. It was a wonderful but scary feeling. Sam walked out of the bathroom in all his beautiful, masculine glory and she found herself blushing in confusion.

"Hey, sweetheart," he said with that easy grin of his. "You look good enough to eat. Now, let's have some fun."

Suddenly he pushed her down on the bed and climbed on top of her, pulling her negligee down and exposing her breasts. For a moment CJ was frozen in horror. Then an unspeakable and irrational terror began to rule her body and her emotions. Like a runaway freight train the terror rushed at her, threatening to overwhelm her. A horrible feeling of suffocation made her think she was going to black out.

"No! No! Get off me!" she screamed as she began frantically to hit him and push him away. Sam was so surprised at her reaction he rolled off her and on to the floor with a crash, knocking the lamp off the nightstand.

Shaking and crying she pulled up her nightgown and sat up on the bed, clutching the ridiculous pink satin sheets to her chest.

"I can't do this. I can't!" she sobbed.

Sam looked up at her from his awkward position on the floor with a puzzled look on his face, which quickly turned to anger. He stood up, towering over her with his face twisted in an ugly snarl.

"What do you mean you can't do this?"

"I don't know why, but I just can't."

"But we're married. You're my wife. Of course, you can do this. I know you've never made love before, but I'll help you through it."

Shuddering, she couldn't even look at her husband.

"No, I can't. Please don't touch me," she pleaded tearfully.

She desperately tried to get the escalating terror under control. Her reaction to Sam made no sense. She had not expected she would react this way to his love-making. Her mind circled around the questions: Why can't I do this? What's wrong with me? I know he is not trying to hurt me. Why am I being so unreasonable?

Then, without another word, Sam grabbed her and threw her on the floor, ripping off her nightgown. CJ screamed and started kicking him, scrambling to get off the floor. Sam grabbed her by the hair and pulled her back toward him. As she twisted around to try and get him to let go of her hair, his fist collided with her face and she crumpled to the floor. She came to a few minutes later, struggling to breathe. Sam was on top of her, viciously raping her.

When she tried to get out from under him, he hit her again and everything went black. When she finally regained consciousness, Sam was gone. The clock on the end table said it was 5 a. m. She groaned as she tried to get herself up off the floor. Every inch of her body hurt. One eye was swollen shut and blood dripped from between her legs as she stood.

Her mind could not process what had happened. Suddenly nauseous, CJ grabbed a sheet off the bed to wrap around herself and tried to walk around the bed toward the bathroom. Suddenly the room started whirling and she collapsed on the bed, tangled in the sheets. Blessed oblivion took her away again and it was 7 a. m. before her bruised and battered body screamed for her to wake up.

As she tried to make sense of what happened, the door to her room opened and Sam nonchalantly walked in, pushing a room service cart with delicious smells wafting from the covered plates and a single red rose in a silver vase sitting on the tray.

"Good morning, sunshine," Sam said. "Hey, you don't look so good. Why don't you take a shower and then we'll go see the sights of Las Vegas?"

CJ cringed as he left the cart and moved over to sit beside her on the bed. The smells from the food suddenly making her nauseous.

"Hey look, sweetheart," he said contritely. "I'm sorry about what happened last night. But you are my wife and you need to understand I have the right to do what I want with you. I didn't mean to hurt you, but you made me do it. Now, how about you take that shower and then we'll have some breakfast?"

CJ couldn't believe he could be so calm about the whole horrible incident. What kind of nightmare was she in? How could she, the director of a domestic violence shelter, be caught in the same web of violence as the clients she worked with every day? What was she going to do?

Sam's smiling face began to change to anger as she sat frozen on the bed. She looked up at him, her mouth gaping in disbelief at his words. He grabbed her by the arm and pulled her to her feet. He didn't raise his voice but the threat in his expression and tone was obvious.

"Didn't I just tell you to get in there and take a shower? Now get going before I have to remind you who the boss is in this family."

Stumbling as the sheet she had wrapped around herself tangled around her feet, her emotions numb and body screaming in pain, CJ limped into the bathroom.

"And don't lock the door," Sam yelled at her as she shut the door.

Trembling so hard she was afraid she would fall, CJ grabbed the side of the sink, dropped the sheet and then carefully maneuvered herself into the shower. As she waited for the water to get hot enough, her mind scrambled for some rationale response to what had happened to her. She was in no condition physically to fight Sam. She was afraid he would kill her if she didn't go along with what he wanted. She stepped into the pounding stream of water and winced as the water hit the bruises on her body. Taking a washcloth and soap, she rubbed her body, vigorously trying to rid herself of Sam's smell, groaning as she touched the painful bruises and rug burns on her body.

Then it hit her. She should not be taking a shower. How many times had she told women not to shower after being raped but to get to the hospital, so a rape kit could be used in order to prove who their rapist was. But Sam was in the bedroom and she knew she could not get past him without a fight; and she was in no shape to fight back.

As the numbness began to wear off and the pain hit with a vengeance, CJ's confused mind whirled with options to get her away from Sam. She let the water from the shower cascade over her head as she scrambled to deal with the difficult and dangerous situation. Maybe if she went along with what he wanted an occasion would arise where she could get away from him. But how was she going to explain the bruises to the shelter's staff and board of directors? How could she have missed signs Sam had such a terrible temper? If she reported the rape and beating to the local police, what would happen? She always believed marriage was forever, but could she stay with a husband who abused her? If she divorced him, would God ever be able to forgive her for making such a terrible mistake?

She didn't realize how much time had passed until Sam barged into the bathroom, sweeping back the cheap shower curtain and demanding to know why she was taking so long. She shrank back against the shower wall and put her arms across her breasts, trying to maintain some semblance of modesty as she felt herself on the verge of panic again.

"I've had my breakfast and now I want to get to the casino," he said, "Get your butt out of the shower and get dressed. You are so pathetic standing there. You look like a drowned rat. Get out of there and try and make yourself presentable."

CJ realized she had no choice but to do as he said. She carefully stepped out of the shower and with her head down moved around him to grab a towel. Sam grabbed her hair as she moved past him and jerked her around to look at him. In a low, menacing voice he said, "And don't even think about running away from me. Don't forget, I'm a cop and there is nowhere you can run I won't find you."

He let go of her hair, strode back into the bedroom and flipped on the television set.

"I'm in great shape this morning," he yelled at her over the sound from the TV. "I was in the casino all night and I'm up $500 from the blackjack table. If I keep it up, I'll be able to pay for the cost of the trip."

CJ emerged from the bathroom, towel drying her hair. As she got dressed in jeans and a t-shirt, she kept an eye on Sam, hoping he would focus on the TV and ignore her. She tried half-heartedly to put some makeup on the bruise forming around her eye, but there was nothing she could do to cover up the swelling. When she was dressed and her long, wet hair was pulled back into a pony tail, she mutely stood by the bed, her head bowed, waiting for Sam's next instructions. She was sure if she said or did anything else he would use it as an excuse to attack her.

After what seemed like an interminable amount of time, Sam stood up without a word and grabbed her arm. She winched at the pain as his tight grasp set a bruise throbbing.

"We are going downstairs to the casino and you are going to be a good little girl and watch me make some big bucks," he snarled.

CJ managed to grab her purse from the table near the door as Sam dragged her out of the room. As they walked into the elevator, another couple stepped to the side to give them room.

"Whoa," the man said as he looked at CJ. "What happened to you?"

Sam tightened his grip on her arm and laughed as he said, "Oh she just ran into the bathroom door last night. She's a real klutz."

CJ kept her eyes focused on the floor of the elevator and didn't say anything. The ride down to the casino seemed to take forever. The other couple sensed something was wrong but didn't say anything more. They knew better than to try and tangle with a man Sam's size.

When she gingerly sat beside Sam at the blackjack table, the dealer looked at her and asked her if she was okay. She must have mumbled something, although later she couldn't remember what she said or anything else about the whole morning. Her mind refused to focus on anything except how she could get away from Sam.

After what must have been several hours, the mental shock began to wear off and CJ began to get angry. Then she started praying silently, asking God to help her. An idea began to form as her body began telling her it was time to use the bathroom. When there was a break in the game, she leaned over and asked Sam if she could go to the bathroom. He grabbed her arm, pulled her over to him and whispered in her ear, "You better get back here in five minutes or you'll think last night was a walk in the park, sweetie."

Struggling to avoid letting Sam know how furious she was, CJ slowly walked toward the bathroom. Fortunately, the door to the bathroom was out of Sam's view so she could walk right past the bathroom and out the casino door. Quickly she hailed a taxi and told the driver to take her to the police station. She glanced out of the rear window as the taxi moved away from the casino and she saw Sam frantically running after the taxi.

"Go faster!" she screamed at the taxi driver. "He's going to catch me!"

Startled at her scream, the driver tromped on the gas and the tires squealed as he just missed a delivery truck crossing in front of them. Thrown across the back seat of the taxi, CJ almost passed out when she slammed into the handle of the door, hitting a particularly large and painful bruise.

Within five minutes the taxi pulled in front of the police station. CJ grabbed her purse, struggling to open the door. Terrified she looked around and was relieved to see no sign of Sam.

He probably thinks I'm too much of a chicken to report him. Although the pain from the rape was a constant reminder of what had happened to her, CJ's numbness and fear now replaced with anger; the next few hours another nightmare. A young, bored rookie cop slowly took her report. He obviously didn't care what had happened to her. Finally, in desperation, she slammed her hand down on the metal desk. He jumped from the sound, giving her a little satisfaction, she startled him from his complacency.

"Look, bozo, I've just been raped and beaten within an inch of my life by my brand-new husband. This is not about jay-walking. Are you going to do your job, and do it a bit more quickly, or am I going to have to talk to your supervisor?"

She was pleased to see she finally got his attention. He sat up straighter and looked chagrined. The processing of her report seemed to pick up a little speed, but it was another hour before she and her bruises were photographed. It was 2 pm before she was gratified to see through the front window a handcuffed Sam being escorted out of a police car. After she identified him as her husband and the one who raped and beat her, Sam was booked and taken to jail.

The burly sergeant who took pictures of her bruises and finalized the report assured her Sam would be in jail for at least 24 hours and she didn't need to stay in Las Vegas: her statement and the pictures enough. He kindly suggested she see a doctor, but she assured him she would be okay and took a taxi back to the hotel.

Even though she was mentally and physically exhausted, she threw her clothes and toiletries into her suitcase, tossing the ripped nightgown into the trash. She grabbed the first flight out of Vegas to Chicago. The plane wasn't full. She was able to sit by herself and avoid embarrassing questions from a seat mate. During the four-hour flight, CJ castigated herself repeatedly for being so stupid as to allow her infatuation with Sam to blind her to what he was really like.

How could I have not seen what he was like? All the signs were there. He was controlling, and I let him take charge. I was naïve and foolish. How am I ever going to explain this whole sordid event to the staff, the shelter board of directors, and my mother? If they find out I got myself into a situation where I became a victim of domestic violence myself, they will begin to question my judgment and my ability to be the director of Safe House. I should not have married Sam without getting to know him better first.

CJ groaned as the plane hit some turbulence. The groan was not just from the jolt to her aching body, but from the dilemma she faced.

Police officers were notorious for sticking up for fellow policeman so there wasn't much chance any charges against Sam would stick. Without her in Las Vegas to stick up for herself, it was doubtful they would believe her over him, but she couldn't stay there and risk him getting out of jail and killing her. Sam was a manipulator and could make people believe whatever he wanted. No, it seemed like there was no choice but for her to immediately file for a divorce and pretend it hadn't happened.

Maybe, once she was back in Fredricks, Sam would be too afraid of her connections in the Village to give her any trouble. If he started hassling her she would go to the police chief, report him and get a restraining order.

As her mind tumbled repeatedly through every incident that had gotten her to this point, she realized she should have made sure Sam was a Christian, although she knew it was no guarantee he wouldn't have beaten her. She also needed to have a long talk with her mother when she got back to Fredricks. There had to be a reason why she reacted with such horror to Sam's love-making, setting off the violence. Maybe if she hadn't reacted the way she had he wouldn't have lost his temper.

Then it hit her: she was rationalizing Sam's behavior just like the battered women she saw every day at the shelter. Tears of pain and rage were her constant companion during the interminable flight. Since their decision to elope was on the spur of the moment, Sam's possessions were still in his apartment. At least she didn't have to deal with his things at her apartment. She figured Sam had gotten out of jail and the charges dropped when a few days after she returned from Las Vegas, Sam was effectively served with divorce papers; which he apparently signed without protest. Maybe her willingness to report him in Vegas had caused him to have second thoughts about coming after her.

Making the decision to file for a divorce went against everything she had been taught about marriage, but she did not believe God wanted her to put her life in danger by staying married to Sam. Her first day back at work was a nightmare. She could only respond to the reasonable questions from the staff about her bruised face and her shortened vacation with inane, nebulous answers. The staff at the shelter could tell something was wrong but didn't press her for details. She appreciated their respect of her privacy and tried to move on with her life. She told her mother and everyone who ask, she'd taken a fall at the motel pool. The bruises on her body began to fade, but she knew her bruised heart was going to take longer to heal.

Until she got her period three weeks after the incident, she wondered if Sam had used protection when he raped her, or if she going to have to deal with a pregnancy. It was a relief to find out she wasn't pregnant, but CJ trembled whenever she caught a glimpse of a tall man, afraid it was Sam wanting to hurt her. Her nightmares were worse after the rape and the familiar, threatening, shadowy figure turned into Sam.

The jumble of cascading emotions related to the rape threatened frequently to spill over into her quiet moments, but she forcefully shoved them away. "I have no time to deal with these things. Eventually the pain must go away. I don't need to keep thinking about them."

She found no harassment notes on her car when she returned from the trip and no phone messages. Maybe the harassment had stopped. She called

Sergeant Rakowski who told her they had traced one of the calls to a prepaid, disposable phone, but it was as far as they got in trying to identify the harasser. He assured her they would keep the case open and to be sure and let him know if the harassment started again. Sam must have said something to him about wanting off the case because Rakowski said he had taken over without giving her an explanation.

A month after the wedding fiasco and rape, she gathered her shattered courage and called her mother and asked her if she could come by for a visit.

"Sure, CJ," her mother said. "You are always welcome, you should know that."

Her mom was living in an apartment in a retirement community and had been very busy with her volunteer work at the church. CJ didn't see her very much. They didn't seem to have much in common anyway so their visits with each other were rare. Her mother's overall attitude seemed to have improved somewhat since the move several years ago. Her health was better, and she even had a smile on her face and glint of happiness in her eyes periodically. CJ was still a bit skeptical whether her mother had really changed, so she was still on her guard during her guilt-driven visits with her mother.

As CJ drove to her mom's apartment she rehearsed her questions: Did Dad abuse me? Did he sexually assault me? Although her father had always been a taboo subject, CJ knew instinctively, as well as from her work at the shelter, her relationship with her father had something to do with her nightmares and her fear of sex. But until she heard the confirmation from her mother she would never know for sure. She knocked on the door of her mom's apartment, mentally girding herself for the confrontation.

"Hi, Mom," CJ said as she gave her a hug. "You look great. Where did you get such a lovely dress?"

She walked into the apartment behind her mother, noticing some pictures finally up on the walls. Otherwise, the apartment was rather Spartan. The furniture was utilitarian and seemed to be a hodge-podge of a Salvation Army, early-attic style.

"All right, CJ," she said as she turned to face her with lips tight and no welcome in her eyes, reminding CJ again of why she didn't like to visit her mother. "I appreciate the compliment, but I am sure the only reason you are here is because there is something on your mind. Let's not beat around the bush, okay?"

Her mother's face went pale when without preamble CJ asked, "Mom, did Dad sexually abuse me?"

"I don't want to talk about it," her mother said as she turned and walked away, her shoulders slouching even further into the familiar depressed attitude.

"Mom, I'm sorry. I know you don't want to talk about it. But I must know. Something is wrong with me and I want to know what happened when I was a child."

"I said I didn't want to talk about it," her mother shouted as she angrily jerked her arm away from CJ who was trying to get her to turn and look at her.

"I married Sam, but I couldn't make love to him, Mom."

Pam whipped around and looked at CJ in shock. "What? When? And why didn't you tell me?"

"It was last month, and we didn't tell anyone because we eloped on the spur of the moment and went to Las Vegas. No congratulations are needed, Mom, because we are already in the process of getting divorced."

Pam sat down in her rocking chair with a shocked look on her face.

"What do you mean you are getting divorced? You just got married! And what were you doing in that terrible Sin City, anyway? I raised you differently than to traipse off to such a horrible place. And how can you get divorced? Divorce is a sin. I can't..."

"Mom, stop!" CJ angrily interrupted her, "I didn't come here to get a lecture on Las Vegas or on divorce. And, in case you have forgotten, you're divorced, too! I came here to ask you what happened to me when I was a child. Why couldn't I make love to my husband? What's wrong with me?"

Suddenly weak, CJ fell on to the worn, ugly couch, the hidden emotions and horror crashed through her defenses and she began to cry. Silently her mother moved to the couch and put her arm around CJ, something she hadn't done in years. As CJ sobbed, her mother held her and awkwardly patted her back, waiting for the tears to work their way through her shuddering body. When CJ began to run out of tears, and the nearby Kleenex box was almost empty, her mother started to quietly talk.

"I guess it's time you knew," shuddering as she tried to find the words to tell CJ what she desperately had hidden from her daughter all these years.

"It happened when you were four years old. I heard you cry out in the middle of the night and so I got up to check on you. I noticed your father was not in the bed but thought he might be downstairs in the kitchen or something."

CJ sat up straight and looked at her mother with dread and anticipation.

"I found him naked in your bedroom. He was on top of you and fondling you in a very inappropriate way, with his hand over your mouth to keep me from hearing your cries.

"Furious, I grabbed your favorite book off your night stand and hit him over the head with it. As he rolled off you with a yell, I started to hit him again. Oh, CJ. I was so angry. I couldn't believe he was doing this awful thing to you."

Her mother started to cry and it was CJ's turn to comfort her mother as she continued the horrible story.

"Your father staggered to his feet. He had obviously been drinking. In fact, there was a half-empty bottle of beer on your night stand which had fallen over and broken when I picked up the book to hit him. He started yelling you were his daughter and he could do what he wanted, and nobody was going to tell him differently. Besides, he was only trying to show you how much he loved you.

"I picked up the broken beer bottle and threw it at him, hitting him in the face. He started bleeding all over everything. He picked up the bottle and started for me, screaming like a demon. But he stopped suddenly when he heard the siren and the screeching tires as the police pulled up in front of the apartment.

"Evidently a neighbor heard the screaming and called the police. He backed off in a panic, grabbed his clothes off the floor and headed for the door. I yelled at him he ever showed his face around us again I would kill him. He ran down the stairs and out the back door. That's the last I ever saw of him. I took you to the hospital, but they said he hadn't raped you. I filed a report with the police, but nothing ever came of it. It was like he disappeared into thin air.

"I bought a gun and kept it close by for years. I divorced your father and we moved out of the apartment in Chicago to Fredricks and into the house on Elm Street. I took back my maiden name, legally changed your name to Pierce, and I hoped it was the end of it."

Her mom shook herself from the memory as she sat up and grabbed CJ's hands. With her head bowed in sorrow she said, "CJ, I never wanted you to know what your father did to you. You never talked about it and I didn't bring it up. I was brought up to believe there are some things better left unsaid. And I hoped you were young enough for it not to affect you. But I see now I was wrong not to tell you. I'm sorry."

CJ sat beside her mother in silence as she tried to absorb what had happened to her and to her mom. She was surprised to notice, rather than anger, she felt relief, relief there was now an explanation for why she couldn't make love to Sam and what was behind her nightmares. She also felt deep sadness for her mother and what she had gone through to protect her. Now she understood so much more about why her mother had been so negative and was often depressed. She realized she had always been very critical of her mom but had never really appreciated what her mother had done to protect her.

"Mom," she said through new tears, "Thank you for what you did to protect me. I understand now why I reacted to Sam's love-making the way I did. It wasn't your fault. You did what you felt was right at the time. I am sorry for not being more understanding."

The two women hugged and sat in companionable silence as they began to assimilate the obvious change in their relationship. CJ felt closer to her mother than she ever had, understanding for the first time so many things about her mother's character and past behaviors. But she wasn't ready to tell her mother about the rape and beating. Maybe someday after she was stronger emotionally she could talk about them, but not now.

Mother and daughter talked for several hours, building a new relationship from the pain of the past. When CJ left her mother, she felt like a huge load lifted from her shoulders. Her steps lighter than for a long time, CJ thoughtfully returned to her own apartment. That night she slept like a baby. The nightmares stayed away and never returned. She called Pastor Neely to get the name and number of a counselor. She needed to get some answers to her questions about marriage and divorce and to make sure she was back on the right track with God. She told the counselor, Karen Wilson, about her father, the rape, and the marriage fiasco. With Karen's help, CJ began to understand in a very new and personal way what domestic violence was all about.

Karen urged her to report the rape to the local police, but CJ just couldn't deal with the stigma and questions which would arise. She agreed to go to her gynecologist to get checked out and to be tested for any sexually transmitted diseases like HIV test, which was negative.

"CJ," Karen gently told her during one session, "If you don't report the rape and the beating, what is going to stop Sam from doing it again to some other woman, or from coming after you again?"

"I know," CJ replied, "but I'm just not ready. If Sam start's bothering me, or I hear he's hurt someone else, then I'll come forward. But I just can't right now!"

CJ started to cry at the dilemma she was in. Karen came and sat beside her on the couch, putting her arm around her and patiently waited for the tears to stop.

"You have to be careful," Karen advised. "Men like Sam are time bombs waiting to explode and you could easily be hurt or killed. Don't put it off too long or someone else might be hurt, too."

CJ took a deep, shuddering breath and looked up from the bunch of soaked tissues crumpled in her hands.

"You're right," she said. "I just need a little more time."

"Okay, CJ, I'll respect your wishes."

During one of the sessions, Karen helped her to look at what the Bible had to say about marriage and divorce. Although she made it clear there were no easy answers and the Bible said marriage was to be a symbol of a Christian's relationship to Jesus, and thus sacred, she also talked about God's forgiveness. One of the most interesting discussions occurred when Karen introduced the concept of church discipline to address battering. CJ looked puzzled as she brought up the topic.

"I know, CJ. Unfortunately, it is very rare for a church to exercise the early church method of dealing with a believer who is sinning. But the Bible clearly states the elders of the church are to meet with the person, if they are a believer, and encourage them to change their ways. So, if a woman is married to a man who abuses her, she should ask the church elders to talk to her husband. The only caution I would issue is in some cases it is better for the women and children to be out of the situation first, like moving to Safe House, to prevent retaliation. Then, if the husband refuses to get help and refuses to acknowledge his sin, then I believe the wife should leave him.

"The church discipline process in the Bible says if a believer refuses to give up their sin, then the church should kick him out of the fellowship. I can't imagine why this same process wouldn't apply in an abusive marriage as well."

"Wow," CJ said as a light began to dawn in her understanding. "It is the first time I've really looked at battering as a sin justifying divorce when the batterer refuses to change his ways. It makes sense. Okay, I can see this, but what about re-marriage for the woman?"

Karen sat back in her chair and was quiet for a minute. "Although I believe marriage is forever, I think each situation has to be carefully and prayerfully evaluated. In some cases, a woman might decide to never re-marry. But, in cases where God brings a godly man into her life, I also believe God provides forgiveness for choices she may have made, such as marrying the batterer outside God's will. I strongly believe God wants us to be safe and happy. Staying married to a batterer is just plain wrong, in my opinion."

After a few weeks of counseling and spending time in the Bible, CJ began to feel stronger and to think seriously about talking to the police about the incident. But the pressures of running the domestic violence shelter soon pushed it away as less of a priority.

Chapter Six

Friendship Renewed

CJ sat in the coffee shop, sipping an espresso while taking a much-needed break from the demands of the CPA combing through the Safe House accounting records in preparation for the annual audit. If she never saw another financial report, she wouldn't mind a bit.

A couple of times a week she would pop over to the coffee shop, which sat on the opposite corner of the town square from the Safe House administrative offices, just to have a change of scenery and to chat with the colorful characters who frequented the shop. She remembered as a child visiting the site when it was a soda fountain, run by Mr. and Mrs. Matouchii. The Matouchii's had retired a year ago and sold the shop. The new owners, Fred and Fern Trinkle, had the appearance of eternal hippies and kept the 1960's décor of her childhood. In keeping with the theme, they called it the "Yellow Submarine Coffee Shop." Psychedelic posters danced across the walls and colorful beaded curtains draped the windows. The coffee and pastries menu included items like "Flower Power Latte," "Aquarius Espresso," and "Bangle Bagels."

More and more artists seemed to be moving into the Village of Fredricks and they were frequent eclectic patrons of the coffee shop. She enjoyed watching the parade of people and periodically traded painting tips with other artists. The coffee shop was an oasis, taking her mind off of the never-ending demands of her job.

She sighed as she sipped her espresso and tried to get her brain to slow down from worrying over the constant barrage of administrative details she knew gleefully paraded down her daily to-do list. On days like today she questioned her sanity in taking the job of executive director. On top of everything else she had a new board member who was driving her nuts. How Justin Reynolds had managed to get on the board was beyond her understanding. She had decided the whole board nomination process was more about politics than it was about selecting the best person for the job.

"Hey, CJ. Why so glum?" Fred asked as he walked out of the back kitchen, wiping his floury hands on his apron. He and Fern were two of CJ's favorite people. They were without pretense. Fred's graying hair formed a monk-like ring around a gleaming bald head, the remaining hair long and in a ponytail. His salt and pepper sideburns merrily traipsed down his cheek to his chin line. His short, stocky frame was always dressed in blue jeans and a tie-dyed t-shirt. Fern was a female version of Fred, her gray hair waist length. She usually wore it tied back with a scarf when she was working in the shop; her peasant skirts and blouses always bright and colorful. Both wore Birkenstock sandals with heavy socks in the winter, adding to their eternal hippy aura.

"Oh, it's nothing, Fred. I'm just having one of those why-did-I-ever-take-this-job moments."

"Whatever do you mean? You have the best job in the world. You get to make a difference in the lives of women and children every day. You couldn't ask for a better job. And, to top it all off, you're good at it!"

CJ decided Fred might be her biggest fan, based on his frequent, flattering compliments. She never ceased to be amazed how many people thought she had a glamorous job. She couldn't count the number of times people at Business-After-Hours, the monthly Chamber of Commerce meet-and-greet, made comments about how rewarding it must be for her to work for a nonprofit. Little did they realize, most days she felt like she was simply putting one foot in front of the other, trying to keep Safe House financially solvent while making sure the programs ran effectively. Never mind the constant battle with the board of directors to keep them focused on their job and not meddling in hers.

"Yes, we have our success stories, but it sometimes seems like a constant battle just to keep the doors open. The other day I was talking to the head of a women's group in one of the churches, who shall remain nameless. When I asked her for a contribution for the shelter, she told me they support missions, not local charities.

"I must confess I stood there with my mouth open. I couldn't believe what I was hearing! Besides, isn't there something in the Bible about missions starting in our own neighborhood?"

Fred might look like an aging hippy, but he was a devout Christian and taught a young adult Sunday school class. He wasn't afraid to discuss difficult issues, which is why he was often CJ's confidant.

"You're right, but there are a lot of so-called Christians who don't want to get their hands dirty by getting involved in something close to home. They would much rather ease their guilty conscience by sending self-righteous gifts across the ocean somewhere.

"You and your staff deserve medals. Believe me. If I were on the board I'd make sure you all get twice what that stingy board is paying you now."

CJ laughed. "I guess I need to make sure you get on the board!"

She took a sip of her espresso and realized it had gone from hot to tepid. She started to excuse herself to get a warm-up, when her cell phone rang. Oh great, another emergency at the shelter, she thought as she flipped open the phone.

"Excuse me a minute, Fred. I need to get this."

He waved a cheery good-bye and headed back to the kitchen.

"Hello, this is CJ."

"Hi, CJ. Guess who this is?"

"Trina?"

"Yep, it's me!"

"Trina! Oh, my goodness! Where are you?"

It was almost two years since she heard from her high school best friend. For Trina to call out of the blue was an incredible surprise and delight.

"You'll never believe this. I have been transferred to Chicago. I move into my new apartment in two weeks. I didn't want to call you until I signed the contract and it was a done deal. Can you believe it?"

CJ felt tears unexpectedly well up in her eyes as she listened to Trina gush over the telephone. To have her best friend back within shouting distance was too good to be true. What a blessing it would be to have Trina close by. The two friends had accepted Jesus Christ as their Savior at summer camp when they were thirteen years old. They shared so much history. It was going to be fantastic!

CJ had chosen not to make close friends with the people in the community, since everyone was either a donor or a potential donor for Safe House. She always felt like her motives for friendship would be called into question: "Does she want my money? Or "Is she going to ask me to be a volunteer?"

She had never been able to bring herself to reach the level of conversational intimacy with anyone like she had with Trina. Then Trina's mother was murdered, and Trina moved to California, ending the intimacy.

"Oh, by the way," Trina gushed, "I got a call from the Fredricks police last week. Their cold case unit did not give up on finding Mom's murderer. I called them at least once a year to check on their efforts. They said Jack, my stepfather, was found in Oregon, but before they could extradite him to Illinois, he died of a massive heart attack in jail. They matched his DNA to the skin the medical examiner found under Mom's fingernails during the autopsy, confirming he killed her. So, I decided to move back to Illinois when the chance came. I know I don't have to worry about Jack anymore."

"What a relief it must be for you, Trina. I am so glad to hear you don't have that hanging over your head. I know it has been extremely stressful for you all these years."

The women excitedly made plans to get together after Trina moved into her apartment and settled into her new job. CJ walked out the door of the coffee shop with a new spring in her step, heading back into the jaws of the audit with an almost cheery attitude.

The only fly in the ointment of her happiness at Trina's news were frequent telephone calls from Justin, the new board member. From the first time she met him, CJ was uneasy around him. She couldn't put her finger on what it was, but there was an uncomfortable familiarity about him. He always stood too close to her, looking down at her with dark, almost black eyes burning with some unnamed intensity.

It was only a week after his election to the board when he unexpectedly showed up at her office. Justin was tall and thin, stoop-shouldered and with salt and pepper hair. His rather gaunt face was accentuated by a nasty scar running from his left eye down to the corner of his mouth. He put his feet up on her desk from the side chair on which he sat, and matter-of-factly told her, "CJ, I have been responsible for getting the executive directors of two nonprofits fired, and you're next."

For a moment CJ could only stare at Justin with a stunned expression on her face. Finally, getting a hold of herself, she calmly asked him, "What do you mean?"

"Well," he said with an incredible air of arrogance, the scar causing the corner of his mouth to curl and make him a appear to be snarling. "I think you are too young for the job for one thing, and I also think you and your staff are coddling the Safe House clients. You keep trying to get them to leave their relationships when you ought to be focusing on helping them repair their relationships. The Bible tells us marriage is a sacred union. Wives who leave their husbands are sinning. The shelter should not be allowing such things as divorce."

Just then Justin's beeper went off. Without giving her a second look, he took off out the door. CJ sat there with her mouth open, appalled at what she just heard. She had never had such a thing happen before. Shakily she called the board president, Albert Finnigan, and told him what happened.

"Oh, come on, CJ. I'm sure you just misunderstood what he said. Don't worry about it. Besides your annual performance review is coming up in another month and if he has any issues I'm sure he'll let me know."

As she slowly hung up the phone, CJ was shaking with anger. She did not appreciate Albert being so dismissive. She had no reason to lie about such a thing. Justin's words were indelibly burned into her brain. Based on Albert's response she would evidently have to deal with Justin on her own. What was it about Justin setting her teeth on edge? And why was he so determined to make her life difficult?

The concerns about Justin ended up getting put on the back burner when one of the Safe House counselors called and told her she was needed at the shelter for a consultation. It was a week after the shocking conversation with him, Justin started calling her almost daily with some type of inane or useless comment. She finally instructed her administrative assistant, Becky Stuart, to screen her calls and to not connect her with Justin when he called.

"When he calls just tell him I am not available, Becky, and I'll get back to him when I can."

She hoped it would take care of the problem. At least if she didn't answer the phone she could pick and choose when she responded to him. Maybe eventually he'd get the idea and quite calling.

It was also the week the harassment started again: the same nasty notes on her car and the same heavy breathing on her telephone. Maybe it was Justin who was harassing her or maybe Sam was behind it, angry at her reporting him to the Las Vegas police and then divorcing him. The community gossip vine said Sam had dated a woman for a while after their divorce, but the girlfriend had a filed a restraining order against him just a month ago. She sighed to herself as she concluded she had to talk to the police about Sam. After the audit is done, she said to herself. And then I need to check and see if there was something in Justin's background which might explain his bizarre behavior toward me."

Becky did the required criminal background check on Justin before his final approval as a board member. Maybe something showed up she overlooked. But after reviewing the documents a second time, CJ couldn't find anything. There was a note in the file indicating Justin said he didn't have an original birth certificate because it was destroyed in a courthouse fire in Moline, but it didn't seem to be enough grounds for suspicion. Apparently, he got a copy of the birth announcement from the Moline newspaper and used it to get a valid birth certificate from a judge.

CJ never heard of anyone being able to use a birth announcement as a substitute birth certificate, but she figured it was possible, especially if the person had political pull like Justin seemed to have. He told her many times how close he and the governor of Illinois were.

After reviewing Justin's file, CJ sat quietly in her office and thought about the situation. It was her word against Justin's and she knew board members well enough to know her word wasn't sufficient for them to remove him from the board. Over the years, she learned the hard way rarely would volunteers fire other volunteers. Volunteers, especially board members, seemed to have huge blind spots when it came to the foibles of other board members. It was her job, she was told repeatedly, to get along with the volunteers.

"I dare anyone of them to put up with what I must put up with board members," she many times grumbled to herself. "I'd like to see them deal with twenty bosses trying to tell them what to do!"

She looked at the file again. Justin was the Chief Financial Officer at Vail Software, a new company which had moved into Fredricks last year, apparently right after the original harassment ended. His application for the board position said he had an accounting degree from the University of Indiana. She guessed his age at about 67. His resume indicated he spent the last thirty years working at various firms across the United States, staying at each company for two to three years.

She met his wife, Alice, at the Safe House annual meeting and felt sorry for her. She seemed to be very quiet and always looked to Justin before she answered a question. As far as CJ knew there were no children or grandchildren. Since the incident in her office a couple of months earlier, when Justin told her he was going to make sure she got fired from her job, CJ tried to adapt to his idiosyncrasies, like she did with every board member. But she instinctively knew something just wasn't right about the whole situation. She made a few telephone calls to places where he claimed to have worked and no one remembered him. Her suspicions grew. She needed to be sure he wasn't who he said he was before she went to the police and to the board of directors of Safe House with her information.

Over the years CJ learned to trust her instincts. More than once she got herself and some Safe House clients out of some pretty sticky situations because she seemed to know when danger was in the air.

The first time her instincts went into overload warning was at a meeting with a client at the Yellow Submarine coffee shop. As she listened to the client talk about needing to file a restraining order against her husband, CJ felt the hairs on the back of her neck stand up and she suddenly had an overwhelming sense of danger. She kept telling herself it was just her imagination. But she was so uneasy she found she couldn't concentrate on the conversation.

"I know this sounds silly," she told the woman, "But I really think we need to go to the police station and file a restraining order right now."

Surprised, but enough on edge herself to understand CJ's unease, she grabbed her purse and the two women headed out the back door to the parking lot. They were just getting into CJ's car when they heard a deafening crash at the front of the building. Totally freaked out, CJ screamed at the woman to fasten her seat belt and they took off for the police station. They found out later the woman's irate husband crashed his pickup through the coffee shop window, right where they were sitting a few minutes earlier. After recovering from his resulting injuries, the husband was convicted of attempted murder and sent away to jail for fifteen years. Since the incident, whenever her instincts started screaming, she reacted without hesitation.

She knew criminal background checks only looked at convictions for felonies but didn't look at employment history. Was Justin who he said he was? Why did she feel so uncomfortable around him? The double whammy of the harassment and Justin's hostility were getting to her. Maybe it was time she did a little amateur detective work. But first, she needed to talk to Pastor Neely.

She was really struggling with what Justin said about marriage, divorce and God's will. If she was going to be effective with battered women, she needed to quit putting off addressing the spiritual side of the issue. She knew she was not living her life for God, as evidenced by what happened with Sam. Maybe it was also time she got things right with God.

Chapter Seven

Murder in the Forest

With Trina's encouragement, CJ joined Fred's Bible study group at Faith Community Church. She enjoyed the interaction with the other members and was encouraged by what she was learning in the Bible. But she still could not bring herself to talk to anyone other than Karen about what Sam had done to her. She wasn't sure if it was because she didn't want other people to think less of her, or if it was just easier to shut down her emotions. Maybe things with Justin would straighten out and the horror she still felt about the rape would eventually go away.

I should have done this a long time ago," she said to herself as she left the Sunday Bible study. I'm learning so much and realizing how much less stressed I am as I draw closer to God.

Her cell phone rang as she reached for the door handle of her car, interrupting her revere. Her heart sank as she realized it was a call from the police.

"This is CJ. How can I help you?"

"CJ, this is Sarge. I'm afraid I have some bad news for you. We found a body on the edge of the forest preserve, behind the shelter. We think it might be another one of your clients."

CJ sagged against the car.

"Are you there, CJ?"

"I'm sorry, Sarge. I'm just trying to grasp what you just said. Do you know who it is?"

"No, but since the body was found so close to Safe House, I'm wondering if you can come down to the morgue and see if you recognize the victim. We couldn't find any ID on her."

"Sure, I'll be right there."

As her thoughts tumbled around with unanswered questions, she drove to the police station. Sergeant Rakowski was just coming out of the station when she drove into the parking lot. He waved her into a spot and beckoned her to follow him as she got out of the car.

"The door to the morgue is around back. Are you sure you are okay to do this? I know looking at dead bodies in a morgue is not a great way to spend your Sunday afternoon."

"I'm glad to do what I can, Sarge. Do you know how she was killed?"

"Looks like she was strangled with some type of wire."

Sarge opened the heavy door and led the way down the steps to the morgue. It was not the first time CJ had been asked to identify a body; unfortunately, too many of the Safe House clients ended up in the morgue. Taking short breaths to try and deal with the strong odors, CJ followed Sarge through the swinging doors. A body, covered with a white sheet, lay on a steel table. The medical examiner, Dr. Chris Stanislaus, standing next to the body, nodded at them and pulled the sheet back. CJ tried not to look at the deep gash on the woman's throat. She gulped and cleared her throat.

"Yes," she said shakily, "She is one of our clients. Her name is Joanne Baker. She came to the shelter yesterday and was going to file an injunction against her boyfriend today."

"You okay, CJ?" Sarge asked.

"Yeah, I'll be okay. What else do you know about her death? Was she drugged?

"It's too early to tell if there were drugs involved," Dr. Stanislaus said. "I'll know more after I get the toxicology results from the lab."

"Come on, CJ," Sarge motioned to the door. "We can talk more in my office. I need to know more about the victim."

"I have to do some more checking on Joanne, Sarge. When she checked into the shelter yesterday, one of the counselors did the paperwork, so I really don't know a lot about her. My guess is the person who killed her was her boyfriend."

She was struck with a sudden thought. Could Sam somehow be involved in this? But it doesn't make sense. Yes, he can be violent, but I don't know if he was this woman's boyfriend.

"Okay, spill the beans, CJ. I can just see the wheels movin' in that pretty head of yours. What are you thinking?"

CJ broke from her reverie and confessed to Sarge what had happened a few months after she met Sam: the marriage, the rape and then the divorce.

"What the H E double toothpicks!" Sarge yelled. "How come you didn't tell me this before?" And what makes you think Sam might be connected to this murder.

"Sorry, Sarge. At the time, I was so embarrassed I married an abuser I didn't want anyone to know for fear it would jeopardize my work at Safe House. Besides, I never heard anything from Sam after the divorce. I just tried to put the whole thing out of my mind. And I don't know if he is connected to this."

"Are there any other little tidbits of information you've been keeping from me? Anything at all? Is there anyone else you have had problems with at the shelter?"

CJ thought for a minute: Nah, Justin couldn't have anything to do with this, could he?

"Fess up, CJ. Out with it."

"Well, I have been having a lot of problems with the board chairman, Justin Reynolds. He thinks we are too easy on the women at the shelter. He is totally against divorce and seems to blame the woman if they are beaten by their husbands.

"I know!" CJ held up her hand to stop the Sarge from exploding. "It doesn't make sense for someone to come on the board of a domestic violence shelter when he feels that way about women. But you know very well, working with the board members of a nonprofit is a lot like the political gauntlet Chief Johnson wades through all the time. I don't usually get to pick who comes on the board or who I must work with as chair of the board. Besides, I just can't see how Justin could have anything to do with the murder. But you asked me if I was having problems with anyone else, so I'm telling you."

"What if this Justin guy has a vendetta against women, especially women who try to get out of abusive situations?"

"I don't know, Sarge. He is a respected member of the community with a good job. Why would he jeopardize that by killing someone? I have my suspicions about his wife being abused, but no proof."

"I don't know what the connection might be either. But maybe he's done this before. How long has he lived in the area?"

"Only a couple of years, I think. He came on to the board last year. We did a criminal background check on him, but nothing showed up. The only suspicious issue is he claims his birth certificate was burned up in a fire at the courthouse in Moline."

Sarge sat back in his chair and scratched his chin. "You've certainly given me some stuff to think about. I'm going to check on both Sam and Justin's background and see what else I can dig up. I'll get back to you, okay? In the meantime, let me know if you find a boyfriend or husband's name for the victim."

"Thanks, Sarge. I can't see the connection between my harassment and the murder, but I guess stranger things have happened. I'll keep you posted from my end, too."

Chapter Eight

Suspicious Circumstances

A few days later, CJ sat on a park bench near the old Moline courthouse, re-reading a newspaper article from June 6, 1973 she copied from a computer search:

The Moline courthouse was seriously damaged last night in a fire which investigators are calling suspicious. Fire Chief Jeffrey Coogan said no one was seriously hurt in the two-alarm fire which started sometime after midnight. One unidentified fireman suffered minor injuries when a portion of the basement ceiling collapsed. Damage from the fire was limited to a section of the basement where old records were kept. Additional water damage in the courthouse lobby will keep the courthouse closed for at least a week, according to Chief Coogan.

Police Chief Tom Richards stated there is evidence someone broke into the back door of the building. Richards is asking if anyone saw anything they should call the crime line at....

CJ sat back for a moment, thinking about what the article said. There were no indications birth records had been destroyed, as Justin stated on his criminal background check application, only "damaged." Why would he lie about something like that, unless he had something to hide? How could she find out exactly what had been destroyed?

CJ told her staff she was going antiquing, but in reality, she decided to do some checking on Justin. She called her mother and Trina to let them know where she was going, without going into any detail. Although she confided to Trina her suspicions about Sam and Justin during a phone call from her apartment before she left, she didn't want Trina worrying about her, so she told her she was going to Moline to look for a new antique mirror for her bathroom.

Trina was settled into her new graphic arts job in downtown Chicago. She and CJ spent several glorious weekends together, catching up on their years apart. It was like they just picked up where they left off in high school. Their friendship was back on the same old easy familiarity CJ missed so much in the intervening years when Trina was living in California. Although they were both busy with their jobs, they tried to get together for something fun at least once a month.

CJ was surprised to find out, while she was in California, Trina made a re-commitment to Christ. She enthusiastically talked about what a difference her new relationship with God made in dealing with her mother's murder and in how she now looked at life. It was good to be able to share with each other their mutual spiritual odysseys. Trina encouraged CJ to continue her efforts to draw closer to God.

As CJ drove leisurely west across the state of Illinois, she wondered if it was time to tell Trina about what Sam had done to her. So far, she hadn't been able to bring it up, not wanting to dampen the rekindling of their friendship. And, since Trina's mother had been murdered, CJ was sure talking to her about the murder of the Safe House client was not a good idea.

CJ arrived in Moline just before dark. Moline was supposedly Justin's birth place. She got a room at the local Holiday Inn and had a surprisingly dreamless and restful night. She asked for a 7 am wake-up call. She wanted to be at the courthouse by the time it opened at 8 am.

She yawned expansively as she flipped back the covers in response to the morning's wake-up call. She stumbled sleepily into the shower, letting the pounding of the hot water wake her up. She slipped into a pair of black linen pants and a white short-sleeve silk blouse, pulling her hair into her usual pony tail. She slipped into a comfortable pair of loafers, applied some light make-up and added a swipe of lipstick to her full lips. She quickly packed her things into the small suitcase, looking carefully around the room to make sure she hadn't forgotten anything, taking the suitcase to the car where she locked it in the trunk. Swinging her purse on to her shoulder she walked to the hotel lobby with brisk steps.

After the continental breakfast in the hotel lobby, she asked for directions to the courthouse and navigated the rush hour traffic to park in the parking lot a few minutes after the courthouse was scheduled to open. CJ doubted seriously if the courthouse in front of her was the same one significantly burned in the early 1970's. It was too new. The modern looking brick and glass, three-story building sprawled at an angle on a full city block east of the river. CJ began to wonder if she was wasting her time on a wild goose chase for information about Justin's background. Maybe the original courthouse had burned down.

She was here now so she might as well ask questions. She walked up the steps into the courthouse. After making her way through the security gauntlet she approached the bored looking young receptionist sitting in a kiosk in the center of the lobby.

"Can you tell me anything about a courthouse fire in the late 60's or early 1970's?" CJ asked.

Not even looking up from her industrious filing of her nails, the woman said she had no clue about a fire and suggested CJ check the old micro-fiche files of back newspapers at the library next door.

Boy, she's a real winner, CJ grinned to herself as she headed out of the courthouse and down the steps to the library.

The librarian was more helpful. She informed CJ there were two courthouse buildings: the new building housing the police department, "the one with all the windows," she said, "and the old gray stone building sitting on the block behind the new one." According to the librarian, the old courthouse was now used primarily for county administrative offices.

The bored receptionist is obviously the star attraction at the new courthouse, CJ thought factitiously to herself. After the librarian showed her how to use the micro-fiche machine, CJ spent the next two hours painstakingly looking through dozens of front page stories, beginning with 1970. Her eyes blurry from the effort, she was just about ready to stop and take a break when the June 6th article slid across the screen.

Bingo! she said to herself. She then quickly did a perusal of articles for several weeks after the fire. The only other article she found indicated the fire department ruled the fire was an arson crime, but the police had no leads as to the perpetrator. Chief Richards stated he believed the fire was probably started by vandals.

CJ's well-honed instincts were screaming, but there was still no proof of anything which might indicate Justin could be a physical threat; at least she didn't think so. The fact people at his previous places of employment didn't remember him could be credited to his only staying at the companies for three years or less, or it could be she hadn't talked to the right people. Claiming his birth certificate was destroyed in a fire was certainly not a crime. And the newspaper article she read was innocuous, with no indication how many or what specific records were damaged.

After re-reading the article, CJ tucked a copy into her purse and walked out of the library. It was a beautiful day, with the late summer heat cooled by a wispy breeze from the river. The library and new courthouse sat on two sides of a well-manicured park dotted with ancient oak and maple trees, their canopies of branches and leaves providing frequent shade. Park benches encouraged the wanderer to enjoy the atmosphere. She could see a small dome perched on top of an old four-story gray building directly behind the new courthouse. As she walked toward the domed building, she stopped to read the plaque on one of several Civil War monuments strategically placed around the park.

Come on, CJ, quit lollygagging and do what you came to do. CJ chuckled to herself as the outmoded word popped into her head. She hadn't thought about it for years, but the word reminded her of an elderly woman who lived next door in the house she grew up in. Every day when she walked to school the woman was industriously sweeping or shoveling her sidewalk – depending on the time of the year. When CJ would stop to ask her if she could help, the old woman would always grumble and say, "Nope. Now you just git and quit your lollygagging around here!"

She smiled to herself at the memory and picked up her pace, walking up the wide steps into the old courthouse. No security gauntlet here. Opening the nine-foot tall heavy brass doors, the first person she saw was an elderly black gentleman pushing a mop around the lobby floor, his curly white hair a stark contrast to his chocolate skin. The dark blue janitor's uniform seemed to hang on his skinny, stooped frame. The receptionist seated inside a large wooden circular desk was busy helping someone else, so CJ sidled over to the man.

"Excuse me, Sir."

The man looked up at her with a hesitant smile. "Hello, young lady. What can I do ya fo?"

"Hi. My name is CJ Pierce. I'm visiting from the Chicago area and I need some information. Do you think you could help me? I'm trying to find out if there was a fire in the courthouse in the late 1960's or early 1970's? The receptionist is busy, and I hoped maybe you might know something."

"Glad to meet ya, Miss CJ. I be Paul Hawkins," he said as he took a hand from the mop, wiped it on his clean and neatly pressed coveralls, and reached out to shake hers. His callused handshake was firm.

"Yes, I 'members dat fire. 'Twas in 1973. Now why in the world woulds ya wants ta know 'bout dat?" he asked her with a curious look.

Silently asking God to forgive her for the lie she was about to tell, she told the story she had rehearsed in her mind while she was having breakfast earlier.

"Well, Mr. Hawkins, my grandfather said he could never get a copy of his birth certificate because it burned up in a fire in Moline. He said not having the birth certificate had created no end of problems for him. He has an 80th birthday coming up and I wanted to see if I could find a copy of his birth certificate somewhere."

"What a nice thing ta do," Hawkins said. "Okay, I don't knows much, but I be glad ta tell ya what I 'members."

"Mr. Hawkins, is there somewhere we can talk more; maybe a coffee shop or something?"

"I tells ya what, Miss CJ; my shift ends in 'bouts 30 minutes. How bouts I meet ya at the diner 'cross the street from dat new courthouse 'bouts leben?"

After they made the arrangements, Hawkins went back to slapping the floor with his mop and CJ headed out the door to the well-worn diner. She found an empty booth close to the door, ordered herself a decaf coffee and Danish and then picked up the scattered remnants of the local newspaper on the red vinyl seat next to her. She decided to pass the time perusing the newspaper, which proved to be a less than exciting look at the lives of the locals, although she did see some ads for antique shops which looked interesting.

Hawkins showed up right on the dot at 11 am. CJ put down the newspaper when she saw him shuffle in, a slight limp giving him a bit of a list to the left. She caught the eye of the waitress who brought over a menu.

"Do you want your usual, Mr. Hawkins?" The waitress asked. Hawkins was obviously a regular at the diner.

"Yep," he replied as he sat down with a sigh in the seat across from her.

"Do ya minds if I has breafast, Miss CJ? It feels like ma stomach's sayin' 'howdy' ta my backbone."

"Please do," she laughed. "And breakfast is on me. I appreciate so much your taking the time after your shift to meet with me. I'm sure you're tired and just want to get home. My mom used to work the same shift, so I know what it's like."

"Why dats mighty kind a ya," he said, his shoulders drooping in exhaustion. He looked like it was well past time for his retirement. "It not be off'n a nice lookin' young woman offers ta buys me breafast!"

She asked him a few questions about his family. He proudly informed her he had seventeen grandchildren, all living in the Moline area. He and his wife, Jennie, still lived in the same house they moved into after they were married some fifty-four years ago. He was retiring next year. Not because he wanted to, but because the county said it was time. He asked her a few questions about her family and then she said:

"Mr. Hawkins, I have a confession to make. My grandfather really doesn't need a birth certificate. In fact, I don't even have a grandfather."

His eyes widening slightly at her admission of a lie, he leaned forward and in a loud conspiratorial whisper said, "Oh, 'twere just ma roguish good looks made yous pick me out ta crowd and offer ta buy ma breafast."

She laughed delightedly. She liked Mr. Hawkins. Then and there she let her instincts rule and decided to tell him the whole story about Justin and her suspicions.

He listened intently, looking down only to attack the breakfast of biscuits, ham, eggs and grits the waitress brought during the story. When CJ finished telling Hawkins everything, where she worked, the harassment, the murders, the shocking threats Justin had made about planning to get her fired, and her instincts that something was off with his story, he leaned back with a quizzical expression on his face.

"Miss CJ, ya truly do has a mystery on yo hands. I has ta tells ya I gots great sympathy fo ya troubles. I be a memba da A.M.E. church, and we had us a right simlar' sit-ye-ation with a preacher few years back. Turns out he weren't who he claimed ta be. He were a shyster tryin' to gets our money. Let me tell ya, we threw him out on his ear."

CJ was surprised at the calm fury in his voice. She was glad she decided to tell him the truth. She was pleased he didn't question the veracity of her story.

Hawkins was quiet for a moment as he thought about her situation. He dunked a piece of toast into his coffee, took a bite, swallowed and then began to talk as he sipped his coffee.

"I jus started da job ats da courthouse in 1973 when dat fire happen'. In dim days da first person da police questions when somethin' like dat happens was da nearest black man. Dat were me. They musta grilled me nigh on ta four hours 'fo they realized I couldn't a done it. Turns out dat fire starts bouts 11:30 pm, 30 minutes 'fo I 'rived fo my shift. One of da policemans was drivin' by da courthouse, saw smoke and calls da fire department so they was able to gets da fire out 'fore it did much damage.

"I stops at a gas station to fills up my truck, on ma way ta work, and one of them policemans happen to be at da station at da same time as me, 'bouts 10 miles outside of town. He gots da call on the fire while we was both pumpin' gas. He 'membered me bein' at da gas station since my momma works fo his family fo years so we knowed each other.

"Anyways, I told 'um I don't know nothin' and they finally lets me get back to ma job at da courthouse. Once them fire and police officials was done with they pokin' 'round, it were ma job to cleans up da mess. I 'member distinctly dat stuff gots burned up 'twere in da older section of da basement. I 'members it 'cause I was bornd in 1936 and all dem half-burned boxes I saw were for da years afta.

"I don't know if dat heps, but dat's what I 'members. Oh, one mo thing. Tooks me severa days to clean up da mess. Dey didn't give me no help so it tooks me a while. On da second or third day I cleanin,' I catch some guy pickin' tru some of dat burned stuff. I yells at him to git and don' think no mo 'bout it. But now I'm thinkin' it coulda been yo guy lookin' for somethin'. Think maybe?"

"Mr. Hawkins," CJ said thoughtfully, "You may have something there. I have no way of knowing if it was Justin, but if it was he might have picked up some information on someone else and has been falsely using it for his own."

CJ sat up straighter as the possibilities whirled through her mind. "He could have stolen someone else's name off a birth certificate or death certificate. Is that where he got the name, Justin Reynolds? Now the only problem is to find out if he was the one who stole it and what is his real name. What did he look like?"

Hawkins closed his eyes for a moment and considered her question. Then, with a twinkle in his eye, he said, "Hard fo me to tell. You white folks all looks alike."

CJ laughed with him. He continued his observations.

"Da only ting I 'members was he a big white guy. I gets no mo dan a glimps a him 'fo he tooks off up da stairs. Didn't report it to nobody 'cause I figgered dey'd not believe me nohow."

"Mr. Hawkins, you have been a great help. Thank you very much."

CJ scooted out of the booth and reached over to shake his hand. On impulse, she leaned over and gave him a peck on the cheek. The smile on his face made her glad she had shown him the affection.

"Oh, by the way, Mr. Hawkins, can you tell me how to get to the cemetery?"

"I knows whats you goin' ta do!" he said as his eyes widened with delight. "You goin' to see if there be a Justin Reynolds buried there!"

He took a napkin and drew a rough map for her of the best way to get to the old cemetery. They said their goodbyes again. CJ paid the check for his breakfast and headed out the door to her car. Mr. Hawkins was still nursing his coffee and toast as she left.

Not sure what she would do with any information she found, she decided it wouldn't hurt to check out the cemetery while she was in Moline. Mr. Hawkins' directions were perfect, and she had no problem locating the cemetery. She found the little shack, exactly as he had described it, where the caretaker sat with his feet propped up on the desk, watching a tiny TV precariously balanced on the window sill, and worrying a plug of tobacco inside his left cheek.

"The Reynolds plots?" he asked. "Yeah, they're over on the southeast corner, right under the biggest oak tree in the place."

Her heart beating with anticipation, CJ drove her car carefully down the little gravel road until she came to the big tree. She parked the car and got out. It rained the night before so the ground around the graves was mushy. Good thing I didn't wear high heels, she thought to herself as she carefully negotiated her way around the headstones and grave markers.

After about fifteen minutes, she found what she was looking for: a small marker with the name "Justin Reynolds, born February 16, 1945, died February 18, 1945, Beloved son of Grace and Henry Reynolds." For a moment, she was stunned at the revelation. But then she realized it proved nothing. There could be more than one Justin Reynolds. The grave only proved there had been a Justin Reynolds, born on the same day as listed in Justin's records. She couldn't remember who was listed on Justin's birth records as parents, but if it was the same as on the gravestone, then it might show he stole the identity. This child died just two days after his birth in Moline.

But what gave her the right to initiate an investigation into Justin? Was she simply looking for a way to keep Justin from his promised effort to get her fired or did she really believe there was something criminal going on? Justin was in a powerful position in the community. Could an investigation into his past result in a lawsuit against Safe House, or against her?

Just in case she might need the information, CJ walked back to her car and pulled out her cell phone. She returned to the grave marker and snapped several pictures.

She was already checked out of her motel so she negotiated her car out of the cemetery and headed down I-80 for Fredricks, her mind swirling with the possible ramifications of what she found. She was so focused on the issue of Justin's identity she completely forgot about checking on the antique shops she saw listed in the newspaper at the diner.

It was almost midnight before she arrived at her apartment. She parked the car in her usual spot and trudged up the stairs. As she put the key into the lock she happened to look up to see the word "Bitch" sprayed in black paint across her door. She hadn't noticed it when she first walked up to the door because her porch light wasn't on. She knew she left the light on when she left for Moline. Puzzled, she reached up and touched the light: it was loose. She screwed it back into the socket and the light came on. Then it hit her. Whoever had damaged her door probably unscrewed the light bulb so he wouldn't be seen. Now her fingerprints probably smudged any prints from the twit who did this.

Double Piffle, she scolded herself. Now what do I do?

Too exhausted to deal with the whole thing, CJ decided to wait until the morning before reporting the incident to the police.

Chapter Nine

Harassment and Murder

It was almost a week after she returned from Moline before she found the time to make the trip down to the police station to report the vandalism on her apartment door and to report to Sarge what she had found in Moline about Justin. There were several hang-ups on her voice mail, so she added them to her list of harassment incidents. The landlord complained about her not painting over the graffiti, but she assured him it would be taken care of before the week was out.

Things had been hectic at the shelter since one of the new counselors resigned while she was out of town; not even giving the customary two weeks' notice before leaving, and apparently unable to handle the daily traumas of dealing with domestic violence victims. So, CJ was placed in the now familiar position of doing double duty: administration and counseling. Fortunately, she still had some contacts at her college alma mater, the University of Chicago, so she called them to see if they had any social work graduates looking for work. Because of the contact she was able to hire a counselor temporarily until she could go through the whole application and interview process.

Today she had to talk to Sergeant Rakowski. The number of harassment calls increased and yesterday she found a big key scratch across the side of her car. She just hoped she wouldn't run into Sam while she was at the police station.

There was a chill in the air as she stepped out of her apartment. It was the first week in September, but it already felt like fall was on the way. She went back into the apartment and picked up a sweater. She couldn't afford to get a cold. There was too much going on. As she ran down the steps to her car, she reached into her purse to take out her I-phone.

I really should call Mom today and then I need to talk to Becky about the design for the marketing materials for the annual Taste of Fredricks fundraising event, she mumbled to herself as she slid into the car and then added some notes to her electronic to-do list.

She looked at her watch and decided she had time to stop by the police station before she had to be at the Safe House office. As she pulled into the police station parking lot, she looked around to see if Sam's corvette was around. Good. No sign of his car so maybe it meant he wasn't in.

After the security check at the door, CJ strode down the hall intent on getting to Jason's office. She stopped abruptly at the sound of Sam's voice behind her.

"Hello there, CJ. Where you been keepin' yourself? Anybody been given you a hard time lately?"

It was the first time they had spoken since the rape and beating in Las Vegas. CJ was pleased to find her heart kept beating at its normal rhythm. But as Sam's last question registered she felt her anger begin to swell. She wasn't sure if he was making an obtuse sexual comment, or if he was talking about the beating or the harassment. Regardless, it was upsetting. Taking a deep breath, she turned and looked at him. He was still a great hunk of eye candy, but she was relieved to find her anger kept her from any other reaction to his physical charms.

"Hello, Sam. As a matter of fact, yes. Somebody has been giving me a bad time. You wouldn't know anything about it would you?" she said with a little hint of sarcasm in her voice. "Because if you are bugging me, I'll nail your hide to the wall so fast you won't know what hit you."

"Whoa, slow down gorgeous! I was just being friendly. You don't have to get yourself in a snit," he said as he backed up against the wall in mock surrender, his hands in the air.

CJ whipped around, her long pony tail conveniently hitting Sam in the face as she headed for the Sergeant's office.

"Ouch," he yelled after her. "You are a real bitch, you know that?"

CJ grinned at his yell, thankful once again she kept her hair long. A girl just never knows when she can use a little extra help to get back at an old flame.

Just then Sergeant Rakowski poked his head out of his office. "Hey, what's all the yelling about?"

CJ sidled past him into his office, mumbling something about men with no intelligence. Rakowski pulled the door closed behind him as CJ plopped into a chair.

"You want to explain what that was all about, CJ?" he asked with a grin.

"Nope. Well maybe," CJ said.

"When you make up your mind, let me know," he replied. "Now what can I do for you?"

CJ slapped the now familiar folder on his desk. "It's started again, Sarge/"

"The harassment?"

"Yes, only it has escalated. I found the word 'bitch' spray painted on my apartment door last week and yesterday somebody key-scratched my car from the front to the back on the driver's side. I get at least three heavy breather calls a day now; never mind the frequent nasty notes on my car windshield. And, what did you find out about Sam?" she asked.

"What makes you think it is Sam?"

"Maybe all of this means nothing," she said with a sigh, "but there was no harassment when I was dating him or when he was dating this other woman. I can't help but wonder if he holds a grudge against me for what happened on our honeymoon and because of the divorce.

"Sarge, I'm not proud of the fact I didn't officially report Sam's rape and beating. I just couldn't deal with the media circus it would cause and how the shelter might be harmed. I know my own hang ups from my Dad's abuse of me are directly related to Sam being so angry with me, but it didn't give him the right to rape and beat me. My instincts are also telling me there is something more to this whole Sam thing than our marriage fiasco. And, whatever it is, it could be part of the harassment episodes and even the murder.

"I checked Joanne's shelter intake file again, and I can't find anything about who her abuser was. The counselor who did the intake said she refused to give a name, which is not uncommon. And, as you know, threats are a regular part of my job. Some disgruntled boyfriend or husband will frequently threaten me because they blame me for taking away their spouse or girlfriend. But, for some reason, this is different than those threats."

Rakowski leaned his bulk back into his chair, which squeaked in protest. He was silent for a few moments as he gathered his thoughts.

"You know you are making some serious charges against a police detective," he finally said, "and because too much time has passed there is not going to be any physical evidence of the rape."

"I know, but I'm sure the Las Vegas police department will have something you can use. Sarge, it has gotten to the point where I no longer feel safe in my home. I have double locks on my door and won't open the door for anyone without first checking to see who it is. I am weary of the whole thing. The constant harassment is starting to mess with my head and it is going to start interfering with my job. I can't afford that right now. Besides, I'm concerned Sam might go after another woman. But it's not just the harassment and Sam I'm worried about."

CJ took a deep breath and with halting words told the Sergeant about the mysteries surrounding Justin and how she thought he was purposely putting her job in jeopardy.

"And, to top it all off," she continued, "the shelter's nominating committee put his name up to be elected as board president for next year."

Once the flood gates had opened on her fears about Justin, CJ told him everything: what she found in Moline, the lack of knowledge of Justin at places where he had supposedly worked, and his threats against her.

"Justin seems to think we are coddling the Safe House clients and we should be working to heal relationships rather than getting the women out of the abusive relationship. His attitude does not bode well for the future of the shelter. All we need is a board president who doesn't agree with the basic philosophy of what we are trying to do. I am afraid for the future of the organization if he becomes president. To top it all off, he has been sneaky about not mentioning his philosophy about Safe House to any of the other board members. So, it is my word against his."

"Have you considered the possibility Justin might be your harasser and not Sam?" Rakowski asked?

"Yes, I've considered it," CJ replied, "and it's one more reason why I haven't come to you before now. However, remember I was being harassed the first time before Justin arrived in the community. I keep wondering if I'm being paranoid about both Sam and Justin. Maybe it really is a spouse or boyfriend of one of our clients who is doing the harassing. I just don't know, but I'm scared. And I don't like being scared. Plus, I can't help but wonder if there is some correlation with all this and the murder, too."

"Okay, CJ, let's get all this written down into a report and then I'll expand the investigation into both guys."

As the ramification of the investigations began to unfold in her mind, CJ began to fidget in her chair.

"What? What's the matter, CJ?"

"I'm just beginning to realize the possible impact on the shelter of any deeper investigations. Justin is a very powerful man. He works for one of the biggest corporations in the county, and one of the major donors to the shelter. If he finds out I'm behind an investigation, I'm toast. And how can you investigate one of your own detectives? Won't Sam go ballistic if he finds out?"

"Trust me; I'll be as discreet as possible. I won't file this report until I've a chance to do a little checking, okay? And can I keep your folder? Your picture of the apartment door and the precise notes on the harassment episodes could be a big help in a prosecution. Oh, I also need the name of the sergeant you talked to in Las Vegas."

CJ let out a sigh of relief. She gave him the Las Vegas information and then handed the folder to him. She reached across the desk and shook the Sergeant's beefy hand.

"Thank you so much for taking me seriously, Sarge. Will you keep me posted on what you find out?

"Sure. I'll call you on your cell phone when I have something. In the meantime, I'd suggest you get an alarm system at your apartment or a big mean dog."

She laughed at the vision of a big dog in her tiny, feminine apartment.

"I think I'll try the alarm system first."

"And, I suggest you make sure you park your car in a well-lighted area, preferably somewhere with security cameras, even if it means you have to walk a bit to get to where you are going. To be on the safe side, you need to either start carrying a gun – be sure you get a permit and some training – or get yourself some self-defense classes."

"Are you sure all that is necessary? I don't like guns and I'd probably shoot myself in the foot if I had one. I haven't really been physically threatened – just a lot of irritating harassment. But I don't want to live in fear, either."

"My experience shows, guys like this usually escalate their behavior when they realize you aren't impacted by their harassment the way they want you to be. You need to do something to protect yourself in case you are attacked. Do you hear me?"

"Okay, okay. I'll think about signing up for self-defense classes. I'll just make sure Sam isn't teaching the class."

Richard laughed at the note of satire in her voice.

As he stood up to escort her to the door, CJ turned and seriously said to him: "Sarge, I have spent my entire professional life dealing with abused women and threatening men. I know the way the law works. Until the abuser does something physical, there is little the woman can do other than file a restraining order. But right now, I can't even do that, since I don't know who is doing the harassing. And I can't do anything about Sam or Justin without jeopardizing the shelter. Once you find out who is behind the harassment, then I'll file a restraining order."

"Good thinking. Now you stay safe, okay?"

Richard handed her his business card after scribbling his cell and home phone numbers on it.

"Call me any time, day or night, if you need me."

"Thanks, Sarge."

Although CJ was still uneasy about where all this might be heading, she felt better having told someone in authority about her fears. Fortunately, she did not run into Sam as she walked out of the station.

She was almost able to forget the harassment as she busily attacked the day's agenda.

Two days later the sergeant's body was found slumped over the steering wheel of his police car: dead from a bullet to his head. The car was parked in a secluded area of the forest preserve and found by a park ranger.

CJ was finishing her breakfast cereal when the morning news broke the story. Dropping the bowl in shock, she sat glued to the television trying to make sense of the whole thing. The reporter said the sergeant was found after his wife reported him missing. He failed to show up at his home after his shift was finished the night before. "More information is pending until further investigation," the reporter concluded.

Terribly saddened at the death of her gentle friend, CJ let the tears slide down her cheeks as she pondered the possible significance of the Sergeant's death. What if her request to the sergeant for an investigation into the harassment, Sam, or into Justin's background is what got him killed? If so, what was she going to do now?

Sergeant Rakowski was the only one who knew about the continuing harassment and her concerns about Sam and Justin. She hadn't told anyone, not even Trina. Now the sergeant was dead. Who else could she trust at the police department? If her suspicions about Sam were correct, the sergeant's death was to his advantage since no one else at the department knew what she told him. If Justin was somehow responsible, how did he find out she talked to the sergeant?

Her mind still swirling with questions, suspicions and fear, CJ wrestled with what she should do next. Just then the telephone rang. Swallowing her tears, she picked up the receiver. It was her mother.

"Oh, CJ, I just heard about Sergeant Rakowski's death. I know his wife from church. I can't believe this has happened. This kind of thing never happens in Fredricks. What is the world coming to?"

"Hi, Mom. Yeah, it's terrible. I knew the Sergeant. He was really a great guy. Hey, can I call you back? I'm going to be late for work if I don't get going."

"Sure, CJ. Are you okay? I mean since you knew him and all."

"I'm fine. Just a little shaken up."

"Okay, I'll talk to you later."

As CJ slowly hung up the phone she briefly considered discussing with her mother the harassment and her problems with Justin. Their relationship had certainly improved since their long talk last year about the sexual abuse by her father, but she really didn't want to worry her mother; she quickly chucked the idea.

In a daze, CJ remembered little about getting ready for work or the drive to the shelter's office downtown. It wasn't until Becky greeted her as she walked into the offices she realized with a start where she was.

"Hey, are you okay?" Becky asked. "You don't look so good."

Pulling herself together, CJ smiled briefly and said she was fine. "I just have a lot on my mind," she said with a wave as she started to walk into her office. "Oh, did you hear about the murder of the police sergeant yesterday?"

They commiserated on the tragedy and decided to send some flowers from the two of them to the funeral. There wasn't enough money in the shelter's budget so they pooled their personal funds for the flowers. The sergeant had been a big help to the shelter since it started and they felt like they needed to do something to let his family know how much he was appreciated. The distractions of the normal, daily hectic schedule gradually moved her thoughts away from the sergeant's death.

It was almost 5 pm before her thoughts returned to the Sergeant. And it was Trina's telephone call which brought everything to the forefront of her mind. Becky put Trina through to her phone and CJ gratefully sat back in her desk chair to talk with her best friend.

"Hey, Trina. You have no idea how glad I am to hear your voice."

"Hey to you, too. What's going on? You sound stressed."

"Look Trina, I really need to talk to you. Any chance we can get together tonight after work for dinner? I know you are still getting acclimated to your job, but I could really use a friend right now. You can come to my apartment if you want. I'll even make chicken Piccata. I also have two pieces left of Mom's apple pie. Can you come? In fact, why don't you spend the night? You don't have to drive back to Chicago tonight, do you?"

"Sure. It's Friday and I was hoping to get together with you this weekend anyway. I'll go to my apartment and pack a bag. I should be there by 7 pm. How does that sound?

"Great! I'll see you then."

CJ hurriedly finished some paperwork and was getting ready to leave when Becky poked her head in the door to wish her a nice weekend.

"I'll lock up, Becky. Thanks for all your hard work this week. See you Monday."

CJ was just walking out the door of the office when her cell phone rang. Before she could even say "hello" she heard a creepy, husky voice say, "You keep your mouth shut or your next." The phone went dead as the caller hung up.

"Now I'm really getting pissed," CJ said angrily as she hit redial. Although she wrote down the number she was sure it would prove to have been made from a disposable phone; just like all the other calls. She shoved the cell phone into her purse and tromped down the stairs.

"Nobody threatens me and gets away with it," she mumbled.

Her mind replayed the caller's words while she negotiated the grocery cart through the store picking up items for the evening's dinner. Somehow, she managed to put together a decent dinner in between peeks at the evening's television news. Information on the sergeant's death was still sketchy, although Police Chief Johnson told a reporter the assailant must have been someone he knew. "The Sergeant was an experienced and savvy cop," Johnson said. "He never would have let someone he didn't know walk up to him and shoot him while he was sitting in his police car. We are putting all of our available resources into finding the assailant."

Just then the doorbell rang. It was Trina. They hugged each other and moved into the tiny living room. Trina plopped her overnight bag on the floor and gratefully collapsed on to the love seat.

"Boy, do I need this!" Trina said with a laugh as CJ handed her a glass of iced tea. "Traffic was horrendous. I guess everyone and their dog are headed north for the weekend."

The stress of the harassment, Sam and the sergeant's death slipped to the background as the two women chatted, continuing to catch up on the time they had been apart. Although they had had several chances to get together since Trina moved to Chicago, it seemed like there were always a lot of stories left to tell. CJ purposely tried to stay away from more serious topics while they enjoyed their dinners and each other's company. She even managed to get some laughs from Trina as she talked about the boyfriend of one of the shelter victims who got lost overnight in the forest preserve trying to locate the shelter. All he knew about the location was it was "near the forest preserve."

"He never even came close to the shelter," CJ said with a laugh. "In fact, when the forest ranger found him the poor man was so distraught he hugged the ranger and swore through his tears he would never set foot near a tree again." Trina hooted with laughter at the vision of a grown man crying because he couldn't find his way out of a forest preserve only a couple of hundred acres in size.

After she wiped her tears of laughter, Trina grabbed CJ's hands across the small table and turned serious as she asked, "Okay, girlfriend, quit putting it off. What's bugging you?"

Gratefully CJ spilled the whole story. For the first time, she told Trina everything about her suspicions about Sam, the marriage, the beating and rape, the problems with Justin, her trip to Moline, the murder of the client, and her anger and grief at the sergeant's death. Tears finally spilled as she talked everything out.

"And just why haven't you told me any of this before now?" Trina indignantly asked. "What are best friends for if not to share each other's woes?"

"You're right, Trina. I should have told you before, but so much of what is going on just seems like suspicions. I really don't have any facts to back them up. I didn't want you to think I was going crazy," she concluded with a shaky smile. "Besides, aren't I supposed to be the strong one?"

Trina frowned at her and took a deep breath. "CJ, we're best friends, right?"

CJ nodded.

"Then what gives you the right to think you are the only strong one? Why should you be the one who must always be strong for everyone? God tells us to share one another's burdens. And by gum, I'm more than a little bit angry you think I'm not strong enough to support my best friend when she is going through this kind of stuff!"

With a start, CJ realized how unfair she had been to Trina in assuming she couldn't handle things. She tearfully apologized and asked Trina for her forgiveness.

Trina suggested they pray about the situation and held CJ's hands as she quietly and gently prayed for God's leading. Tears came to her eyes as CJ found peace and comfort as she began to turn the situation over to God. At one point in their prayers, CJ could ask for God's forgiveness for ignoring God and marrying Sam. As the burdens rolled from her shoulders and she experienced God's forgiveness, CJ renewed her commitment to allow God's leading in her life.

The two friends talked for several hours about the situations and although they did not come up with any solutions, CJ realized later she felt better just having someone to talk to about the whole mess.

Saturday the women spent the day strolling through an arts and crafts show in Mundelein. The distraction was good for them. They agreed ahead of time to keep their cell phones turned off. They wouldn't be interrupted and could enjoy the time together.

Later in the afternoon as they sat in a quaint café eating their deli sandwiches, CJ turned on her phone; just in case there was an emergency at the shelter. The phone beeped, indicating a message, so she checked the voice mail.

"CJ, this is Chief Johnson. It is important I talk to you as soon as possible. Please give me a call. It's about Sergeant Rakowski's murder."

She stood up to move away from the noise of the crowd. "Trina, I'm sorry, but I have to call the Chief of Police."

Trina nodded her agreement and continued sipping on her latte as CJ made the call. She was surprised at how quickly the Chief answered the phone. Apparently, the number he gave her was his cell phone.

"Chief, this is CJ Pierce. You called me about Sergeant Rakowski's murder?"

"Thanks so much for returning my call. I have some questions I need to ask you and I don't want to talk about it over the phone. Can you come in to the station?"

"Sure, Chief. I'm in Mundelein right now, but I can probably get there in about thirty minutes. Will that work for you?" They decided to meet at his office.

It wasn't until she hung up, she realized she would need to take Trina with her, since she left her car at CJ's apartment. Trina eagerly agreed to go with CJ, rather than go by the apartment first.

"No way am I going to let you do this alone," Trina said firmly.

The women paid their checks and quickly drove back to Fredricks. They discussed the possible reasons why he wanted to see CJ.

"He probably found something in Sarge's files about the harassments," CJ concluded. But she wasn't sure about the ramifications of telling her suspicions to the Chief. If she revealed everything and Sam was somehow involved in trying to solve the murder, he would probably find out. Besides, there was no guarantee the Chief would even believe her about the issues with either Sam or Justin. They finally agreed the harassment was something going on for a while so there were undoubtedly records of her reports. CJ decided to just give him the bare facts and nothing about her suspicions regarding Sam or Justin unless he asked.

As they drove up into the police station parking lot, Sam's convertible was nowhere in sight. CJ breathed an inward sigh of relief. She didn't want to run into him again. And she certainly didn't want Trina to meet him. Sam would undoubtedly hit on her and CJ wasn't sure how she would feel about it.

After negotiating the security system, the two women walked through the station, Trina looking around her with interest since it was her first visit. Several of the detectives on duty gave her the once-over, but in her usual way Trina totally ignored their stares of admiration.

"Things haven't changed much," CJ joked to Trina. "You still get all the looks from the boys and I'm invisible." Trina playfully hit CJ on the arm and laughed as they headed down the hall toward the Chief's office.

The Chief saw them approaching through the glass windows of his office and beckoned them to enter. CJ introduced him to Trina and he gestured for them to sit.

"Can I get anything for either of you? Coffee? Water?"

"No thanks," they said at the same time, grinning to each other at their duet response.

"Before you get started, Chief, you probably should know Trina knows everything about what has been going on; you don't have to worry about her being in on the conversation."

"Okay then," he said as he sat back in his chair. "Here's the deal. One of the detectives was going through some papers in Sarge's patrol car and found your name and phone number. Was he working with you on something, or was it about the harassment you reported last year?"

"I was in to see the Sergeant a few days ago," CJ said, tears beginning to well up as she realized again her visit might well have caused his death. Steeling herself to the task at hand, she sat up straighter, cleared her throat and continued.

"The harassment has started again, and it is getting worse. Sarge said he was going to look into it."

"Do you have any idea why he wouldn't have filed a report on your complaint? I can't seem to find one in the files anywhere."

CJ looked quickly at Trina before she continued, thinking carefully about her words before speaking again. She was uncomfortable bringing Sam's name into the discussion. She asked instead, "Could he have regarded the original report from last year as sufficient?"

The Chief frowned as he thought about it. "It's not like Sarge to neglect putting new information to the old report. But, I guess it is possible. Okay, tell me more about the harassment. I want to see if there might be a correlation between your harassment and his murder."

Speaking matter-of-factly, she told him about the folder she had given to the sergeant and summarized the most recent episodes: the key scratch on her car, the word spray-painted on her apartment door, the continuing heavy breathing on the telephone and the notes under her windshield wiper.

Taking a deep breath, she decided on the spur of the moment to tell him about her suspicions related to Sam and the possible correlations with

Joanne's murder. But she left out any reference to Justin, afraid the Chief would think she was paranoid.

The Chief sat forward in his chair, looking intently at her but he didn't say anything until she was finished.

"I told Sarge about the beating and rape. He wrote it down on a report and then he took the folder where I had recorded each of the harassment incidents. Did you find the report or the folder?"

"No, they are not in his office or in his car. Anything else you need to tell me?"

"I guess the only other thing I need to tell you is about the telephone call I got the day after Sarge was killed. The caller told me to keep my mouth shut or I'd be next."

Chief Johnson's normally stoic face showed a moment of surprise and then the mask dropped over his face. "I don't like the sound of it."

"So, where do we go from here?"

"Is there someone with whom you can stay while we investigate this further? I don't want you to take a chance on you being the perpetrator's next victim."

"Chief, I appreciate your concern. But I'm not going to hide from this nitwit. I'll be careful, I promise. I'm used to dealing with creeps. It's part of my job at the shelter. I'll be fine."

Just then Trina spoke up. "Why can't you stay with your Mom?"

"Mom's health is not the greatest. And besides, she lives in a senior community where someone under the age of 55 can only stay for 30 days. I just don't think it will work. But, if it will make you both feel better, I'll check on it. Okay?" knowing full well she would not do anything about it.

"CJ, you need to be careful," the chief said firmly. "This is not some ordinary kook. This guy is dangerous. And I am going to get an internal investigation going on Sam. Do you want to file a restraining order on Sam?"

She thought for a minute, took a deep breath and agreed. She filled in the necessary forms and then gave the Chief the information on the Las Vegas incident. After assurances to the Chief she would be careful, CJ and Trina headed out of the Chief's office. As they stepped out of the station, headed for the car, Sam roared up in his Corvette, screeching to a halt in front of them. CJ groaned, "Just what I need, run-in with Sam."

Trina's eyes widened as he unfolded himself from the car. "You were not kidding," she said out of the corner of her mouth to CJ, "he is one hunk of sweet eye candy."

"Well, would you look at this; two beautiful women gracing the steps of our illustrious police station. To what do we owe the honor?

"Come on Trina," CJ said with a hand under Trina's elbow, starting down the stairs. "We have better things to do than chat with the local riff-raff."

Sam let out a hoot of laughter, but never took his eyes off Trina.

"Aren't you going to introduce me to your friend?" he asked with a grin.

"Sam, this is Trina Larson. Trina, this is Sam Harris. Now come on, Trina, we have things to do," dragging the apparently reluctant woman down the stairs.

As CJ slammed the door on the car, she rounded on Trina angrily. "How can you bat your eyes at that piece of garbage after what he did to me?"

Trina's eyes widened in disbelief at CJ's bitter words.

"Sorry, CJ. I didn't realize you still had feelings for him. Besides, all I was doing was admiring how he looks. For heaven's sake, I'm not interested in him. So, get off your high horse and settle down! Besides, after what he did to you I'd much rather kick him where it hurts the most!"

Mollified, CJ shrank against the seat of the car. "You're right. I'm sorry. I'm being a real putz. Every time I see that man I just want to bite nails."

There was silence between them as CJ started the car and pulled out of the parking lot. CJ knew their brief spat was over, however, when Trina started making goggle-eyes at an elderly gentleman hobbling down the sidewalk with cane in hand. He stopped in his tracks, his mouth open as he watched a gorgeous woman make silly faces at him. He turned slowly as the car picked up speed, never taking his eyes off Trina.

"You are so mean," CJ laughed. "You'll probably give the poor guy a heart attack."

By the time they arrived at CJ's apartment, they were back to their old comfort zone with each other. Trina had already told CJ she would have to head home in the evening, since she didn't want to contend with the weekend traffic returning to Chicago on Sunday.

"Thanks, Trina, for listening to all my woes. You are the best of friends."

"No problem-o, CJ. You just be careful. I couldn't stand it if something happened to you. I'll be praying for you."

The women hugged and CJ walked Trina to her car, promising to keep her posted on the whole harassment thing. She waved until Trina was out of sight, then walked glumly back to her apartment.

On Monday CJ hired a security firm to install motion sensitive alarms inside and outside of her apartment, including a video camera over the front door.

Tuesday CJ received a telephone call which shook her world.

"This is the charge nurse at Highland Park Hospital. Are you CJ Pierce?" an unknown voice asked.

"Yes, this is CJ. What can I do for you?" Fear spiked through her body.

"I'm sorry to have to tell you but Trina Larson was seriously injured in a car accident yesterday. It took us until today to get your name from her employer. She has you listed as her emergency contact. Are you a family member?"

CJ's heart stopped for an instant.

"Is she okay?"

"I can't give you this kind of information over the phone. Are you a family member?"

"She doesn't have family here. Her closest relative is in California. Can I see her?" CJ asked in desperation.

"Since she has listed your name as her emergency contact, we can talk to you if you come to the hospital. And you need to come soon."

CJ's hands were shaking as she wrote down the information on the location of the Highland Park Hospital. After she hung up, she called her mother and told her what had happened. Her mother insisted on going with her to the hospital and CJ gratefully accepted the offer. She wasn't sure if she could handle this on her own.

Shooting prayers heavenward for Trina's recovery, CJ grabbed her coat and purse and rushed out of the office, informing Becky she had a family emergency and wouldn't be back for the rest of the day.

When she and her mother arrived at the hospital, they asked for directions to the intensive care unit. CJ introduced themselves to the ICU charge nurse and ask if they could see Trina. Taking them into a consulting room, the nurse informed them Trina was stable but still in serious condition.

"You can see her for ten minutes, but she won't respond. She's in a coma from a serious head injury."

"Can you tell me what happened?" CJ asked shakily.

"Apparently she was driving home from the grocery store when she was run off the road. Her car hit a telephone pole. If she hadn't been wearing a seat belt she would probably be dead."

Later the doctor informed her there was no way of knowing if Trina would ever regain consciousness and, if she did, whether or not she would have severe brain damage.

The next few months were a blur of short visits with the unconscious Trina. The Aunt in California was recovering from a stroke and was unable to make the trip to Illinois, so CJ was her only frequent visitor.

CJ struggled to keep from going into a deep depression. The incidents of the past several months were almost too much to bear, so she decided to set up some sessions with Pastor Neely when she found out Karen was out of town.

"First, Sam rapes and beats me, a woman from the shelter is murdered, the Sergeant is killed, and now Trina's life is in danger. I don't know how much more I can take. Do you see a black cloud hanging over my head or something?" CJ facetiously asked Pastor Neely as she sat in his office with her head in her hands.

She minced no words as she told him about her marriage to Sam. She also told him about her renewed faith in God but the struggles and questions she still had about God's sovereignty when it came to battered women. And she was finally able to talk about the murders: Trina' Mom, Joanne, and now Sarge.

For the next hour Pastor Neely helped CJ to take a more objective look at what was going on in her life. As the session ended, he walked over to sit beside CJ on the sofa and said, "You work in an extremely stressful job, CJ. You see the results of violence in individual lives every day. You know you can only do so much to help them.

"In the same way, look at your own life and what's happened and ask yourself how much of what has happened is your fault and how much must be laid at the feet of the perpetrators. Don't forget, while God could intervene, we are all responsible for the choices we make. When we fail to consider God's will in our relationships, sometimes we must suffer the consequences.

"And, no, I don't believe God intends for a woman or her children to stay in an abusive situation. God's grace and forgiveness are for everyone. Divorce is not the unpardonable sin."

With those words, CJ sighed deeply and sat back.

"I know you are right," she said. "Thanks. You've given me a lot to think about."

She left the session encouraged and strengthened personally and spiritually; ready to address the next issue life threw at her.

Chapter Ten

An Awakening and a Death

It was Christmas Day. There were pathetic attempts to decorate the hospital with tacky garlands and the periodic Charlie Brown Christmas tree, but nothing could change the distinctive smells and sterile environment of the hospital, CJ thought, as she stepped off the elevator on the third floor. Trina was moved to a recovery room a few weeks earlier, although she still showed no signs of coming out of her coma. She thought seriously of dumping the small Christmas stocking with Trina's name on it which she carried; Trina wouldn't know she brought it anyway.

With a sigh and second thoughts, CJ pulled the stocking away from the garbage can and carried it with her into Trina's room. The only thing left of the jungle of tubes and wires surrounding Trina after the accident was the feeding tube. She was pleased to see Trina's beautiful red hair was starting to grow back. Her head was shaved for surgery to reduce the pressure on her brain from swelling. As she gently picked up Trina's hand, her eyes popped open and she looked straight at CJ.

"Nurse! Nurse!" CJ screamed as she dropped the ridiculous stocking and frantically pushed the call button. "She's awake!"

Several of the nursing staff rushed in at the sound of CJ's screams. As they realized what happened, they quickly checked Trina's vital signs. One of the nurses rushed out to find the doctor on call. CJ stood beside the bed in awe as Trina's eyes never left her face. She leaned forward to listen as Trina tried to talk around the feeding tube.

Trine mouthed the words, "Where am I?"

"Oh, Trina, you were in a car accident. But you're going to be okay now, I just know it!"

Not for a moment letting go of Trina's wasted hand, CJ unashamedly wept huge tears of joy and relief. Trina's brow furrowed as she tried to get CJ to understand what she was trying to say. After several attempts at understanding, CJ thought Trina was saying, "Sam."

Trina mouthed the words again: "Sam."

"What are you trying to say?" CJ asked in horror. "Don't leave me, Trina?" CJ begged, terrified as Trina's eyes closed she was slipping back into her coma.

The doctor stepped in as Trina closed her eyes.

"Trina! Trina!" He said loudly. "I can't let you sleep yet. I'm going to remove the feeding tube and then I want to ask you a few questions. You can sleep all you want afterwards."

After removing the tube, Trina was better able to respond to the doctor's questions testing her memory and responses. Then, with great difficulty, Trina managed to make herself understood.

"Truck...shoved...me...off... road...Sam...driving...why?" Trina asked plaintively, and then her eyes started to close.

"Sleep...tired," Trina croaked and then she was asleep.

The doctor gave instructions to the nurses on changes in her care. He took CJ's arm and steered into the consulting room. It was clear from the big grin on his face Trina was going to be fine.

When she finally left the hospital, she pulled out her cell phone and called Chief Johnson, telling him what Trina said. Although he was shocked, he told her to keep the information to herself and he would put out an APB on Sam. When she got home, she called her mother and gave her the good news about Trina and what Sam had done. There was a moment when she felt like what had happened to Trina was her fault because she had told the Fredricks police what happened in Las Vegas.

But after listening for God's leading as she prayed, she felt at peace as she realized what happened was Sam's responsibility. Trina was going to be fine! She went to bed and slept for eighteen hours, her exhausted body finally relaxed enough to sleep after almost three months of constant shuttling between the hospital and her job.

She awoke to the incessant wringing of her doorbell, followed by a horrendous pounding on her front door. Bleary-eyed, she grabbed a robe and stumbled to the door. She peeked through the safety hole on her door and stepped back in fear at the sight of an obviously irate Sam at the door.

"Let me in, bitch!" he yelled as his foot connected with the door.

Terrified, CJ ran to the telephone to call 911. As she picked up the receiver, the door fell open with a crash and Sam stumbled into the apartment. The security alarm began to shrill in protest. He grabbed the phone out of her hand, tearing the cord from the wall. He threw the phone across the room, putting a gouge in one her paintings hanging on the wall.

Gathering up her robe, she frantically ran for the bedroom, hoping to lock herself in before Sam could get to her. But before she could get the door shut, Sam barreled into the door. CJ fell, banging her head on the hardwood floor. Dazed, she weakly tried to fight back but he kicked her in the side causing her to double-up in pain. The room began to spin and go dark. It was only the beginning of his attack. He beat her furiously, his fists flying and connecting with various parts of her body with sickening thuds. As the world around her began to recede as she lost consciousness, she could hear Sam yelling repeatedly, "I told you to shut your mouth! Why are you making me do this? I told you to shut your mouth!" As things started to go black, she thought she saw Sam pull something out of his pocket.

It was the last thing she remembered until she awakened in the hospital emergency room, the pain from the beating reverberating through every inch of her body. She groaned and closed her eyes, hoping it was all a terrible nightmare. She tried to swallow, but her throat burned like fire.

"Can you hear me?" a voice asked from a distance. "Tell me your name."

"CJ Pierce," she heard a voice whisper, and then the world disappeared again.

The next time she awakened, she became aware of the fact she was in a hospital bed and her mother was sitting in a chair next to her. Confused for a minute, CJ tried to make sense of where she was and why. It wasn't until she tried to sit up the pain brought everything back and she remembered what happened.

"Don't try to get up, honey," her mother said gently. "You have some broken bones and a concussion. You need to rest."

"Sam. What about Sam?" sudden fear causing her to begin trembling.

"It's okay, CJ. It's okay. Sam is dead. He won't bother you or Trina anymore."

CJ fell into a dark hole of oblivion and didn't awaken again until the next day. A doctor standing over her, holding her chart.

"Well, look who is back in the land of the living," he said with a grin. "How are you feeling?"

"Like I've been hit by a truck. How do you think I feel? Now, when can I get out of here?"

"Whoa, take it easy. You're not going anywhere for a few days. You have a broken leg and a fractured arm, bruising to one kidney, a bad cut around your neck, and various contusions, besides the concussion. You need to give your body time to heal."

After the doctor left, CJ started to look around the room but found she had to move her head slowly to not be overwhelmed by dizziness and nausea. She was surprised to see the room was full of flower arrangements and get-well cards. Just then her mother walked into the room.

She bent over and gently gave CJ a hug, tears evident in her eyes.

"Oh, CJ, it is so good to see you awake. I have been so worried about you."

Painfully, CJ tried croaked out some questions. "What's been going on while I've been in here? Who sent all these flowers? What happened to Sam? How is Trina? I feel so bad about what happened to her. If I had reported the rape and beating when I first returned from Vegas, maybe she wouldn't have been hurt. Oh, and is everything okay at the shelter?"

Her mother laughed at the barrage of questions. "You are obviously on the road to recovery!" She sat down and proceeded to fill her in on everything.

"The flowers are from board members, staff and a whole slew of your clients and friends. Trina is fine. In fact, they are letting her go home next week. And don't blame yourself for what happened to Trina. She certainly does not blame you. Sam is the one responsible. And everything is fine at the shelter. Now as to Sam…"

For the next half hour, her mother filled her in on what happened with Sam; some of it gathered from news reports and some from the excited neighbor who talked to her when she stopped by the apartment to pick up some things for CJ. The police issued a warrant for Sam's arrest after CJ's call about him causing Trina's accident, but he eluded them until a passing policeman saw his Corvette in the parking lot of her apartment complex. The officer called for backup.

As two more officers arrived, the 911 operator informed them a neighbor called to say, "a big man is breaking down an apartment door" in the complex, giving the apartment number. Now they had an apartment location, they drew their guns and ran up the stairs. They saw the broken door and rushed inside. They advanced carefully while yelling, "Police! Drop your weapon!" Suddenly there was the loud crack of a single gunshot. They found Sam sprawled on the bedroom floor with a self-inflected gunshot to the head, his blood all over the unconscious CJ. He had killed himself before he could finish strangling her.

Detectives later searched Sam's apartment and found a recorder. Listening to the tapes led them back to CJ's apartment where they found a listening device planted under the lampshade in her living room.

"That's how he found out I told Trina about the beating and rape and my suspicions he was the one doing the harassing," CJ told her mother.

Her surprisingly patient mother waited until now to ask CJ about the rape and beating, so in halting words she told her mother about the terrifying episode leading to Trina's accident and Sam's death. In the telling, CJ began to realize God's protection and forgiveness.

It wasn't until the next week when she was home recuperating, she had a visit from Chief Johnson. Her mother, who spent her days at the apartment helping CJ adapt to her crutches, let him in and started to retreat to the bedroom to give her some privacy for the conversation with the Chief.

"Stay put, Mom. I want you in on this conversation, too."

The Chief informed them they found a folder among Sam's things, the one she gave to Sergeant Rakowski, and a stolen gun matching the caliber of the one used to kill the Sergeant. They also found some wire suspiciously like the wire used to murder Joanne, and identical to the wire Sam used to strangle CJ.

"As near as we can figure," the Chief said, "Sam shot Sarge because he was afraid he was going to be exposed for beating, raping and harassing you. Trina became another victim of his attempt to keep people silent about the whole thing."

"But why was he harassing me?" she asked. "We're divorced, and I didn't report the rape and beating until long after the harassing started."

"We'll probably never know for sure," he replied, "but we found out the Chicago police department received stalking and harassing complaints about him shortly after he went to work for them. They evidently just wanted him out of their hair so they kept it quiet when we checked with them for references.

"If we had known about his violent history we never would have hired him. Interviews with the women he stalked show a pattern of harassment and intimidation before and after dating them. There were also two unsolved murders in the precinct, very much like Joanne's murder.

"Oh, and by the way, we were able to connect the dots between Joanne and Sam. Sam was her boyfriend; the one she filed a protection order against. The only reason we didn't know about the order was because it got hung up in the court system."

"It wouldn't surprise me at all to find out he grew up in a home where his father abused his mother," CJ said sadly and then paused with a quizzical look on her face. "Wait a minute, Chief. You said he stalked the women BEFORE he dated them?"

"Yes, why?"

"The harassment started before I met Sam and stopped while we were dating. He told me he saw me at a fundraiser. Maybe he figured the harassment would place him in a position to be assigned to my case."

Her face went white as she realized how close she had probably been several times to being killed by Sam. She would never know why he had not tried to kill her when she first got back from Las Vegas. He was certainly capable of it, given what they knew now.

"You may be right. Oh, one more thing," Chief Johnson continued. "Can you explain the note we found in the folder which mentions a Justin Reynolds?"

She thought for a moment and decided it would make no sense at this point to go any further with her concerns about Justin. It was clear Sam, not Justin, had been harassing her. She would just have to figure out how to deal with Justin on her own.

"Richard must have written down his name when I was throwing out names of possible harassers. He is a board member I've had problems with but I doubt seriously if he had anything to do with it."

After assuring the Chief she didn't want him to pursue any further investigation into Justin, he left. With her mother's help CJ began the long, slow process of recovery.

Chapter Eleven

Congratulations and Another Murder

It was CJ's first day back at work after Sam's attack and death. Two months passed, and the horrible crutches were now gone. Although her right arm still pained her periodically, the orthopedic physician assured her she would have full use of the arm within a couple of months; if she did the required therapy. It seemed to take forever for the ugly bruises on her body to change from black and blue to a sickly green, yellow, and then finally to fade away.

Her empathy for shelter clients greatly increased because of her relationship with Sam. Even though she knew Sam was dead, her heart still jumped in fear whenever she saw a tall, blond man. During her recovery, CJ spent a lot of time studying the Bible and getting a much clearer idea of God's righteousness, justice and forgiveness, all traits helping her better understand why things like domestic violence and murders occurred and why God did not always intervene.

The staff at the shelter were fantastic. They all did extra duty to fill in for her while she was gone. And Becky did a great job taking care of the administrative functions. She staffed the board meetings, too; a task she told CJ she never wanted again.

"I don't know how you do it," Becky told her. "I'm so glad you are back. Those board members could drive anybody crazy."

CJ laughed as she remembered saying pretty much the same thing to Sadie when she first started working with the board. As she sat down behind her desk on her first day back, she considered how best to get back into the swing of things. Justin was elected the board president, an event she was unable to influence while she was recovering. Now she had to figure out how to work with him and keep him from changing the whole vision and mission of the agency. She was brooding over the situation when Becky informed her Trina was on the phone.

"Trina! How are you doing?"

"I'm fine. Sorry to bother you at work, but I wondered if you felt up to a visit this weekend. I have some great news for you."

Since the two women were both recovering from their injuries, there had been little opportunity to get together other than by phone. The thought of finally being able to spend some quality time with her best friend was immensely cheering. They decided Trina would spend the weekend at her apartment. Trina refused to spill the beans about her "great news," so CJ contented herself with the thought of the weekend.

The rest of the day was spent reconnecting with board members, some who dropped by the office to wish her well and some she talked to on the phone. She saved a call to Justin for last. He was coldly indifferent to her attempt to build some bridges between them.

"I'll call you when I'm ready to plan the agenda for the next board meeting," he said and abruptly hung up.

"Why thank you for asking, Justin. I'm doing well, despite the fact someone tried to kill me," she said facetiously to the dial tone. With a sigh, she tackled the last bit of paperwork for the day and headed home.

It didn't take long for her to get back into the routine of the management of the shelter. Before the week was out meetings began to pile up on her calendar. She was pleased to find the financial condition of the shelter was better than it had been for a couple of years. Apparently, her beating grabbed the sympathy of the public. The result was an influx of funding from people who had never given before.

Her first board meeting after her return was scheduled for the day after the annual "Taste of Fredricks" fundraiser, a month away. The spring food and wine-tasting event was always a lot of work, but it brought in new donors and greatly enhanced the public's awareness of domestic violence issues.

She decided the best way to avoid a confrontation with Justin before the board meeting was to e-mail him a sample agenda and let him make the changes. Once the board meeting was over she knew she would have to have a heart-to-heart talk with him. There was no way she could avoid it. The future of the shelter could well depend on her ability to deal with him.

Although she found herself tiring more easily than before the beating, she made it through the week of work, falling exhausted into her bed every evening. She couldn't wait for the weekend to relax and catch up with things with Trina.

Trina rang the doorbell at 7 pm Friday evening, on time as usual. The two friends hugged and chatted eagerly over Chinese take-out. CJ couldn't believe how good Trina looked. Her short, curly hair formed a halo around her pale face. She is positively glowing, CJ thought to herself.

"Okay girlfriend, what's going on? You look entirely too happy."

Trina grinned. "Oh, you noticed, did you? I'm getting married." She thrust out her left hand, showing off a glittering beautiful diamond ring on the ring finger.

CJ's mouth dropped open in surprise and she began to sputter in confusion. "What? Who? When? How? And what an absolutely gorgeous ring!"

"You are the first person to find out. Do you remember the handsome doctor who took care of me in the hospital? Well, we started dating after I was released from the hospital, and he has asked me to marry him. Can you believe it? I am so excited I can hardly sit still. And, best of all, he is a Christian and wants to establish our relationship and our marriage on Christian principles. It has happened so fast, I haven't even had a chance to catch my breath, let alone tell you about it. Talk about a whirlwind romance!"

CJ hugged her friend and made the appropriate exclamations of joy. The women spent a delightful weekend discussing wedding plans. CJ, of course, was going to be the maid of honor, Trina said, so she wanted her help on everything. The wedding would be held in the early fall.

After Trina left Sunday afternoon, heading back to her Chicago apartment, CJ found herself a bit envious of Trina's happiness. "Oh well," she sighed to herself, "Maybe someday my prince will come."

The weeks leading up to the fundraising event were jam-packed with meetings and last-minute details, which helped to dampen her worries about Justin. The next day after the "Taste of Fredricks" the front page of The Daily Chronicle featured a picture of her with Justin holding a check for $50,000 from his company. She was reading the article under the picture when her mother called.

"Good morning, honey. Great picture of you in the paper."

"Thanks, Mom. It was a very successful evening. We think we may have raised over

$150,000 at the party – the largest amount ever raised at the event. I'm really pleased."

"I know you are probably really tired, so I won't keep you. But I have a question. Who is the man in the picture? He looks familiar."

"Oh, he's the new president of the board, Justin Reynolds. He is the chief operating officer at one of the local software companies. He's the one I told you about who has been giving me problems. You've probably seen him around town. Why do you ask?"

"Oh, nothing. Just curious. Look I must run. Maybe we can get together for lunch today?"

"I'd like that Mom, but it's going to have to be tomorrow. I have a board meeting at noon today."

As she hung up the phone she wondered why her mother's sudden interest in shelter business. They never talked much about her job because she still thought CJ could do better at a different job.

Mentally shrugging her shoulders, she turned to the business of finalizing the myriad of arrangements for the board meeting. Justin agreed by e-mail to meet with her after the board meeting. Although apprehensive about the meeting, she was determined to do whatever she could to make things work for the next year while Justin was president.

The meeting went smoothly with the board completing the agenda items in less time than usual. They were all in a good mood because of the way the previous night's event had gone so there was less dissension than the normal. CJ had to admit,

Justin knew how to keep the board on task and to not get sidetracked on irrelevant details.

As the board members trailed out of the conference room, she said her goodbyes and then told Justin she was going to use the restroom before their meeting. He settled himself into a chair to wait for her, a cup of coffee in his hand and his back to the conference room door.

As she stood in front of the restroom mirror, taking deep breaths to steady her nerves before the meeting, she asked God to give her courage and wisdom in the meeting to come. She was jolted from her revere by the sound of a large thump coming from the nearby conference room. She thought she heard footsteps down the hall, but then, no other sound. Her danger instincts on high alert, she quickly wiped her hands on a towel and poked her head out the door. There was no one in sight. She opened the heavy conference room door and, for a moment, could see no sign of Justin. Then she saw his arm on the table, his coffee cup tipped over next to his hand. Alarmed, she walked around his chair to see him slumped face-down on the table, blood dripping down the back of his neck from a huge gash on his head.

"Justin! Justin! Are you all right?"

He wasn't moving. Terrified, she reached over and tried to shake him. With a thud he fell over, the chair tipping him out on to the carpeted floor. CJ screamed and jumped out of the way. Blood spattered on to her clothes when he fell. Unable to find her cell phone in her usual spot in her pocket, she realized she left it in her purse in her office. Bolting down the hall, she started screaming for someone to call 911. Somebody in the bank must have heard her because in a few minutes the police arrived. They found her in a daze sitting in a chair near Justin's body.

The first police officer to enter the room put on a pair of gloves and reached under the conference room table to pick up what appeared to be the murder weapon, a trophy Safe House had received for a parade float several years ago. The bottom of the trophy was bloody.

It was four hours later, after a lengthy interrogation at the police station, before she stumbled into her apartment. Her mind reeling, and her body exhausted she couldn't seem to focus on anything. She wandered aimlessly around the apartment until she found herself in front of her telephone, staring blankly at the blinking red light indicating a message. Numbly she picked up the phone and dialed her voice mail.

"This is Mrs. Foster, the administrator at your mother's complex. Please call me as soon as you get this message. It's urgent."

Overwhelmed by the barrage of crisis and exhausted from the day, it took her a moment before the words registered. Trembling, she dialed the number and waited for the next horror to hit her. She didn't know how much more bad news she could handle. Silently she asked God to give her strength.

Mrs. Foster said her mother had suffered a stroke and was transported to the Sumter Memorial Hospital. She never could remember how she arrived at the hospital or when she called Trina, who arrived at the hospital within an hour after CJ. Now on auto-pilot, she heard the doctor as though from a distance, saying her mother suffered a heart attack and a stroke. It looked like she would survive, he said, but there were preliminary signs of severe paralysis on her right side. It would mean months of therapy before she could function on her own. Only time would tell if she would ever regain her speech.

During the days and weeks which followed, with God's help CJ managed to find inner strength she didn't know she had. Trina was there to help and encourage as often as she could get away from her job. CJ discovered her mother made prior arrangements so if anything caused her to be incapacitated she would be cared for at the care center portion of the retirement complex where she lived. The news took a great load off CJ's mind, knowing her mom was being taken care of and all financial arrangements had been made ahead of time. Although her mother was unable to communicate with her, CJ told her how much she appreciated her thoughtfulness in deciding ahead of time. The frustration and anguish in her mother's eyes at not being able to talk understandably just about broke CJ's heart.

Once she knew her mom was doing okay, CJ reduced her daily visits to weekly. The flurry of decisions needing to be made after Justin's murder kept her occupied at work. After the board voted the past president in as the president things began to calm down.

Chapter Twelve

Arrested

Two months after Justin's murder, she was working late in her office when the shriek of a police siren outside the bank pulled her away from a particularly puzzling accounting problem. She could see reflected on her wall, the red and blue flashes of the lights flashing in the alley behind the bank. She got up from the desk and looked out the window. She was surprised to see two police officers, led by Chief Johnson, tromping up the back stairs of the bank. The bank was closed so she couldn't imagine what was going on. Suddenly there was a loud knock on her office door. As she opened the door, the Chief stepped into the room and signaled the other officers into the room.

"What's going on, Chief?" she asked in bewilderment.

"Claudette Pierce, you are under arrest for the murder of Justin Reynolds. Anything you say can and will be used against you in a court of law."

As he stated her Miranda rights, another officer pulled her hands behind her and slapped on handcuffs.

"I don't understand. Why are you arresting me?" CJ asked in bewilderment.

Without another word, the Chief and the officers grimly marched her down the stairs and shoved her into the back seat of a police car. The awkward position of her arms created an unrelenting pain in the arm broken in Sam's beating. She could handle that kind of pain, but the emotional pain threatened to overwhelm her. Hysteria would have been her grim companion all the way to the police station if her prayers had not given her strength.

When the booking sergeant asked her if she wanted to make a telephone call, Trina was the only person she could think of to call. Her voice trembling from the stress, she choked out the situation to her best friend. Shocked, Trina assured her she would be there as soon as she could.

"Why don't you wait for morning," CJ suggested, even though inside her head she screamed, "Come now!"

She took a deep breath and shoved aside the screaming voice. "They told me I won't be officially charged until I go before a judge tomorrow. You really can't do anything tonight."

"Do you have an attorney?" Trina asked.

CJ had to think for a moment. She knew a lot of attorneys but only as donors to the shelter or as legal aid for shelter clients. Somehow, she didn't think approaching one of them would be in the best interests of the shelter; too much potential for conflict of interest for them. Then it hit her.

"Chris Neely might be willing to help me. He's Pastor Neely's son. I don't know what kind of litigation he handles, but could you please call Bert? He's the pastor at the Faith Community Church in Fredricks. Ask him to call Chris. If Chris can't help me, he'll know someone who can."

Trina agreed to call Pastor Neely and after some encouraging words and telling CJ she'd be there tomorrow, she hung up.

CJ had enough sense to refuse to answer any questions without her attorney present, so the interrogation lasted only a few minutes. She was then strip-searched by a grim-faced female guard. Her humiliation was complete when she was forced to take a shower with a disinfectant soap making her eyes burn and her skin itch. The Spartan underwear was too big, and the pant legs of a neon orange jumpsuit were too short. So, they gave her a men's jumpsuit too big for her small frame but long enough, making her look like a hobo. Ridiculous paper shoes completed her fashion ensemble. She was none-too-gently thrown into a holding cell.

There was no one else in the cell with her. She wondered if maybe it was because they regarded her as a threat to other prisoners: an ironic and ridiculous thought. She was sure she wouldn't be able to sleep a wink all night. She began to pray, asking God to give her the courage she needed. Her mind was abuzz with questions as to why she had been arrested for Justin's murder. She knew she hadn't done it, but apparently there was evidence pointing to her.

Although the Chief knew she had problems with Justin, she couldn't imagine how he made the leap from irritation to murder. From pure exhaustion, she finally laid down on the thin mattress of the wall-mounted bed, sure she wouldn't be able to sleep a wink. It seemed like her head had just hit the pillow when it was 7:30 a. m. and a guard nosily arrived with her breakfast.

After she picked through the tasteless mound of scrambled eggs and sausage, CJ tried to freshen up with the prison issue toiletries. It was 9 am when a new guard, one as dour faced as the last night's guard, without a word, handcuffed her and escorted her back to the interrogation room. She was in such a shocked emotional state after her arrest she hadn't paid much attention to the surroundings during her first visit to the room. Now, somewhat rested, she could think more clearly about the whole mess. She almost laughed at the predictability of the room: stark, gray walls, a single table and two uncomfortable looking chairs. There was even the requisite large mirror on the wall, undoubtedly two-way. The guard silently handcuffed her left hand to the chair and left the room.

A few minutes later Chief Johnson walked into the room with a short, stocky, hard-faced woman who looked like she was in her mid-forties. Her kinky graying hair was cut very short. Her skin was a dark, chocolate brown. CJ thought she recognized her as one of the first African-American police officers in the county. She couldn't remember if she was one of the officers who arrested her the night before; the event was still a blur in her memory.

"Good morning, CJ. This is Sonja Tipton, the lead detective on this case. She has some questions for you. Are you ready to get started?"

Sonja sat down in front of CJ and the Chief started to leave the room. He turned as CJ said, "Get started with what, Chief? I am not answering any questions until my attorney gets here. I know my rights."

"Come on, CJ," Detective Tipton said quietly. "It will go much easier for you if you cooperate with us from the beginning. And why would you need an attorney if you haven't done anything wrong?"

The Chief made no comment and left the room. CJ turned her attention to the detective.

"Don't you find it odd, CJ, how violence and turmoil seem to follow you around? First the Safe House client, Sarge, and then Sam; and now your board president was murdered. Although there is no evidence you committed the other murders, this murder is one of the most open and shut cases I've ever seen.

"You had motive, means and opportunity to murder Justin, and your finger prints are all over the murder weapon. I'm going to make sure you don't get away with this murder. Mr. Reynolds was a prominent member of this community and the Mayor wants this case over and done with."

CJ sat back in the hard chair, struggling to keep a handle on her emotions. It wasn't her fault all those people were killed. And it was ridiculous anyone might think she would kill a board member just because he irritated her. As for her prints being on the trophy evidently used to kill Justin, of course her prints were on it. She picked it up every time she had to dust the credenza on which it sat. Like the directors of most small nonprofits, her job often included such mundane tasks as clean-up. But she was afraid if she said anything at all she just might make her situation worse. So, she made a zipping motion across her mouth, and folded her arms across her chest, sitting back on the chair.

Exasperated, the detective stood up and slammed her chair against the table. She stomped out of the room, leaving CJ alone with her fears and unanswered questions. Two hours later, about the time CJ decided she could not possibly sit in the hard chair any longer, besides needing to use the bathroom, a female guard took her to the bathroom and then to a different room down the hall, a duplicate of the room she just left; only this one did not include a two-way mirror. "Looks like they are trying to break me with incredibly boring décor," she thought facetiously to herself. And there, standing up to greet her was Chris Neely. She had a brief thought about how handsome he was, but the stress of why she was seeing him unceremoniously shoved the thought into oblivion.

She tried to shake his hand, but the handcuffs made it difficult. "Lora," Chris said quietly, after reading the guard's nametag, "do you think you could remove the handcuffs? She's not going anywhere."

The guard shrugged and removed the cuffs. CJ waited until the guard left before she said anything to Chris.

"Thank you so much for coming," she said tremulously. "I couldn't think of anyone else to call. All the other lawyers I know are donors to the shelter and I just didn't think I could ask them to help me. I don't even know if you are the kind of lawyer I need."

She gratefully slumped into a chair and tried to keep from crying at the sight of someone who might be able to get her out of this horror house.

"I'm glad I can help, CJ," he said firmly. "I would have been disappointed if you hadn't called me. And, yes, I am the kind of lawyer you need. I am a defense attorney with a lot of experience in murder trials. I work for Legal Aid in Chicago. Do you have any questions about my credentials before we get started?"

Assuring him she trusted him to help her through the ordeal, Chris then spent the next few minutes outlining for her the process she would be going through: the arraignment, the bail setting and the preparations for a trial.

"Now, fill me in on what you have been told so far. By the rules of evidence, the prosecutor is required to give me everything they have against you, so once I see what they have we can begin to work on your defense. But right now, I need to hear what you know. How did the police connect you with the victim and who is he?"

With pointed questions prompting her responses, Chris could get from her the whole story. His yellow legal pad was soon full of his notes.

When she finished speaking, Chris set back thoughtfully.

"Well, it appears their evidence is purely circumstantial. The police have connected a bunch of dots, but it doesn't look to me like they have an airtight case. I'll know more after I see their evidence. In the meantime, we need to get you in front of the judge for your arraignment and bail-setting. You are scheduled to appear before the judge at 4 pm. Hopefully we can get bail for you and then you won't have to spend another night here. How much can you put up to post bail? Or do you have someone who will post it for you?"

"I have a little bit in savings," CJ responded despondently. "My mother is in a rehab center after a stroke. I don't have anyone else who might post bail. How much do you think it will be?"

"I don't see how the prosecution could possibly think you are a flight risk, but in murder trials the bond could be anywhere from $150,000 to $1 million."

CJ's eyes widened in disbelief at the ridiculous amount for bail, and the dormant feelings of panic leaped to the forefront of her psyche. "Chris, you know I can't possibly come up with that much. And how am I going to pay you? What am I going to do? I need to get back to the shelter. I need to make sure my mother is okay. I have got to get out of here!"

Chris put his hand on her arm. "CJ, calm down. Don't panic. You don't have to come up with the whole amount; usually it's just 10% of the bail amount, plus something to be used as collateral. And I'm hoping they won't set the bail too high, considering the fact you have no criminal record. As for my pay, we'll talk about it after we get you out of here. I'll check with my Dad and see if he knows some of the shelter board members who might be willing to post bond for you. In the meantime, I want you to re-think everything that has happened and see if you can come up with anyone who might have wanted to kill Mr. Reynolds."

CJ swallowed her tears and the panic threatening to engulf her. Chris changed the subject and got a list from her of toiletries and books she wanted in case she had to spend another night in jail.

"Becky at the shelter has a key to my apartment, Chris. Oh, and my best friend Trina, the one who called you, is on her way here. Could you please give her the security codes for the front gate of the apartment complex and for my apartment's security?"

CJ wrote the codes down for Chris and then ask him if he could have Becky check on her mother. "Becky and my mom get along really well and she sometimes goes to see her. But please, ask Becky not to say anything to my mom about what's happened. I don't want to upset her."

Chris agreed. "I'll have Trina make sure your apartment is locked after she picks up the personal items for you. I'll also talk to Becky. Oh, before I forget, I want to check on which judge is on the docket."

He pulled out his phone and called the court clerk for the information.

"Good," he said after he hung up. "You have Judge Stephen Joseph. I've heard from my Dad he is good and will insure you get a fair trial."

He then reviewed for CJ what would happen at the arraignment hearing in the municipal court and explained the various plea deals the prosecution would probably offer: manslaughter, first-degree murder or second-degree murder.

"I am not going to bargain for any plea deal," CJ said indignantly. "I cannot believe God would want me to plead guilty for something I didn't do."

"Okay, I had to tell you what your options were. I'm glad to hear you are willing to go to trial on this. I hope it doesn't get that far and we are able to get the charges dismissed. However, if it goes to trial, remember, it is not our job to prove you're innocent. It is the prosecution's job to prove you are guilty beyond a reasonable doubt. Now, the only thing you have left to do today is to go back into the interrogation room with me to answer Detective Tipton's questions. But first, let's see if we can get you some lunch."

"I'm not hungry, Chris. Can we just get this over with, please?"

Chris stood up and went to the door to call the guard, who put handcuffs back on her. He helped her up. "I'm right here, CJ," he whispered as he grabbed her arm to catch her as she stumbled when she shakily stood up.

The interrogation was in many ways what CJ had seen on television dramas: the detective asking both subtle and pointed questions, moving from a soft to aggressive approach and then trying to be CJ's friend. There was even an attempt to intimidate her when the Chief entered the room and stood against one wall, not saying a word. When an answer from CJ might incriminate her, Chris was right there to interrupt and say, "My client does not have to answer that question."

Despite the fear lurking like a dark shadow, CJ kept her answers honest, short and calm. She didn't elaborate, regardless of the detective's efforts. CJ could tell the detective was frustrated at her inability to get any incriminating answers.

After three hours of intense interrogation, Detective Tipton sat back in her chair and asked, "Are you sure there isn't something else you want to tell me about your relationship to Mr. Reynolds, CJ?"

She sensed the detective was trying to get her to say something important to solve the case, but for the life of her, CJ could not imagine what she could say to make the nightmare end. She wearily shook her head. Not a good idea. Now her head was swirling from lack of food and stress and she felt weak and disoriented.

"For the last time, and like I told you umpteen times before, the only relationship I had with Mr. Reynolds was as the director of Safe House. Justin was a member of the board of directors and president of the board. That's the only relationship I had with him. I don't know what else I can tell you."

Smugly the detective looked at CJ and said, "You mean to tell me you didn't know Justin Reynolds was your father?"

Time stood still for CJ as what the detective was saying tried to make it through her shocked brain and into her consciousness. Chris frantically reached for her as CJ tumbled off the chair as her body slumped in a faint.

When she came to, she was lying on the floor of the interrogation room with Chris and the detective looking down at her. Detective Tipton was waving smelling salts under her nose.

"Where am I?" was her first bewildering thought. And then the last words of the detective threatened to overwhelm her, and the room began to swirl again.

"CJ! Stay with us!" Chris yelled. "Come on!"

The shock began to recede, and their blurry faces began to crystallize. With Chris' help, she gingerly sat back on the chair and put her head on her knees. That was a first. She never fainted before in her life; must have been from the lack of food.

Justin Reynolds was her father. Now she understood why he seemed familiar. The scar on his face was a result of her mother's efforts to rescue CJ from his sexual abuse thirty years ago. As the reality of her relationship to Justin began to sink into her very soul, CJ felt a baffling mix of anger and sadness: anger because there were so many things she wanted to ask him and couldn't now, and sadness because now she had no chance to ever get to know him as her father. Did he know who she was or was it just an ironic twist of fate they ended up in the same town? If he was the abuser her mother insisted he was why in the world would he want to be on a domestic violence shelter board?

"CJ, are you okay?" Chris asked gently.

She nodded and then looked over Chris' shoulder, her eyes meeting those of the detective. From the expression on her face, it was clear Detective Tipton realized either CJ was an incredible actress, or she really did not know Justin was her father.

Shakily, CJ asked the detective, "How do you know he was my father?"

Tipton cleared her throat and got her facial muscles under control as she explained, as a standard procedure, they took DNA samples from Justin's body and then used a search warrant to get some hair from CJ's hairbrush in her bathroom at the apartment. When they compared their DNA, it was a clear match.

"How come you didn't know he was your father?" Tipton asked.

Before CJ could answer, Chris objected to the question and indicated the reason would undoubtedly come out during the trial.

Tipton shrugged and concluded the interrogation at his request.

"Are you going to be alright, CJ?" Chris asked after the detective left the room.

"Yeah, I'm just trying to absorb the fact Justin was my father."

"I have a private detective friend I'll call to get her working on finding out more about his background.

"CJ, I hate to leave you here, especially after the shocking news you just got about your father, but I have to see Becky and Trina and get your personal items; then I'll try and make arrangements for your bail and be back here in time for the 4-p.m. arraignment."

CJ assured him she would be alright. Chris left and CJ was escorted back to her prison cell where she received a limp turkey sandwich wrapped in Saran wrap and some tepid iced tea. As she sat on the hard bed eating her bland lunch, her head against the wall, she thought back on all her contacts with Justin. She didn't know if she could ever think of him as her father. How could she not have known who he was? Shouldn't there have been intuitive knowledge in her? It was true she was uneasy around him, but she attributed it to his brusque and cold manner. She was four when he left, but surely there was something about him which should have triggered a memory of him as her father.

Wait a minute. His name was Justin Reynolds. Her mother let it slip one day, before she changed CJ's last name to "Pierce," her married name was Douglass. So, she was right. Justin Reynolds was trying to hide his real identity. Her trip to Moline was not a shot in the dark. Her intuition about him was correct. He stole Justin Reynolds' identity. But the detective did not mention the identity issue. They must know, but why did they not tell her about it? She was going to have to talk to Chris.

She closed her eyes and tried to make sense of it all. Could his mousy wife have killed him? She exhibited all the typical signs of having been abused; looking to Justin before she replied to questions, keeping her head down and sticking close to him all the time. Her body language was the same as a victim of domestic violence. But she seemed too beaten down to have done something so lethal. And she didn't look like she was strong enough to have killed Justin with one blow. Or maybe there was someone in Justin's past who had it in for him. If he could abuse a child and steal somebody's identity, there is no telling what else he might have done during the last thirty years. The frantic twisting of her thoughts finally became so tiring she dozed as she sat against the wall, her head bobbing on to her chest.

At 3:45, the noise of the guard unlocking her door awakened CJ. She stumbled to her feet. Lola the guard gave her a few minutes to freshen up as best she could at the tiny sink and warped mirror and handcuffed her again and shackled her feet together. A small gang of police officers marched around her as they escorted her down the hall and out the door. As she exited the jail, she was shocked to see a large crowd of reporters and television cameras surge toward her.

A calliope of shouting voices, the intrusiveness of a dozen microphones and the flash of cameras caused CJ to flinch as the phalanx of law enforcement shoved their way through the throng to a waiting police car.

"CJ!" one reporter yelled, "Why did you kill your father?"

Other voices shouted similar refrains, but CJ put her head down and refused to comment as silent tears coursed down her cheeks at the unfairness of the whole mess. Nothing she could say would make any difference to the mob looking for a story. She was unceremoniously shoved into the back seat of the car. Since the courthouse was only a block away, the trip was a short one and the reporters arrived as CJ exited the car at the back of the courthouse. Another group of officers surrounded her, protecting her from the media frenzy, and then marched her through an unobtrusive door.

The courthouse was familiar to CJ, since over the years she accompanied hundreds of women as they went through the court system, fearfully testifying against their abusers or responding to false accusations of child abuse filed by the spouse in a fit of anger.

Typical of courtrooms built during the New Deal era of President Roosevelt, Grecian columns stood in the front of the three-story façade. Over the years, the white columns faded to a dirty gray. One large courtroom sat directly behind the large brass front door with two smaller courtrooms on the north and south sides.

CJ was now inside the smaller courtroom on the south side in a holding area for the prisoners. The room was about twenty square feet, with three enclosed sides and a clear Plexiglas barrier about 15 feet high on the open side facing the right side of the judge's bench. Wooden, backless benches sat in rows, like a backwoods church gathering. The walls were white, causing the orange of the prison jumpsuits to glare like neon signs. She was one of three prisoners in the holding area.

Lola gestured CJ to sit. The two other prisoners, both male, slouched in boredom on one of the back benches. When she walked in, they both sat up and whistled at her appreciatively, but the guards standing nearby glared at them and they returned to their boredom. CJ sat on the front bench and tried to still her racing heart by looking around the courtroom. Although she had been in the room many times with shelter clients, this was the first time to see it from a prisoner's viewpoint.

To the right of the prisoners' holding area, about eight feet in front of the elevated judge's bench, sat the attorneys for the prosecution and the defense behind large wooden tables cluttered with files and laptop computers. CJ's eyes immediately found Chris, who sat by himself at a table. He gave her a nod and an encouraging smile. Sitting at what she concluded was the prosecution's table was District Attorney Donald Percy. She winched as she remembered the last time she saw him. She gave him an earful because he refused to prosecute an abuser who beat up his girlfriend twice. Percy claimed it was her word against her boyfriend, since she waited too long to report the abuse and the bruises had faded too much. Percy didn't think the yellow-green bruises counted, for some reason.

Percy was nearing retirement. His mane of white hair gave him a distinguished look, but CJ had experience looking down into his steely gray eyes – he was only 5'6" tall - and she knew he would spare no effort to see her convicted of this crime if for no reason other than spite, since he knew she was not in the least intimidated by him.

Why is it short men have such a need to put me in my place? CJ thought to herself; which started her mind down a totally irrelevant track related to the issue of intimidation. With a start, she pulled her thoughts back to the DA. He was known as the Silver Fox and never lost a conviction in a murder trial. There were rumors he cut some ethical corners to get some of the convictions, but he never received a reprimand from the Bar.

Because of his legendary prowess as a prosecutor, and probably because he served in the position so long, Percy knew everybody who was anybody in the community. It was rumored he had thought about running for the Illinois senate early in his career, but quietly withdrew his nomination. The domestic violence rumor mill said it was because thirty years earlier his first wife accused him of battery. But, since he was never convicted, he kept his post as assistant DA. Twenty-years ago he was appointed to the top position of DA. Two of Percy's assistants sat on a bench behind him, by all appearances looking like acolytes for The Great One. Percy didn't even look her way.

Directly behind the attorneys' tables were six long rows of hard, wooden pews filled with family members, the media and spectators, and separated from the attorneys by a four-foot-high barrier covered in wood paneling. The pews were full, so more people stood, crowded around the walls of the spectator area. As her eyes roamed over the spectators, she was touched to see Trina giving her a tiny wave and an encouraging grin.

There was no jury box, since juried trials were held in the large courtroom. The ceilings throughout the courthouse were at least 20 feet high. Noisy fans constantly struggled to push hot or cold air down into the courtroom, depending on the time of year, and usually failing miserably. All furnishings were dark oak, polished so many times they shone from the light streaming in the tall windows scattered around the top of the walls within a foot of the ceiling.

CJ looked longingly at a patch of blue sky she could see through one of the windows, when she was startled by the bailiff's booming voice announcing the entrance of the judge. She was glad to see Judge Stephen Joseph was in fact on the bench. He was always fair and consistent in his dealings with shelter clients and did not hesitate to reprimand attorneys who did not appear to be doing the right things for their clients.

Her case was first on the docket. CJ stood as her name and case number were called and the guard escorted her to the front of the holding room where a microphone stood. As her case number was called, Chris also stood up. He introduced himself and then asked the judge to waive bail.

"My client has no criminal history and is a respected member of the community. She is not a flight risk or a threat to the community. We respectfully request the court she be let out of jail on no bond. She has obligations both personally and professionally which necessitate her being allowed to fulfill her responsibilities and she lacks the financial resources to be able to come up with bail."

"Welcome to our courtroom Mr. Neely. I think you will find, even though we are not like Chicago where you are used to working, I will adhere to the law and I will not allow grandstanding. Is that clear, Mr. Neely?"

"Yes, your Honor," Chris replied quietly and firmly.

Judge Joseph looked toward the DA for his response to the request for no bail.

"Your Honor," Percy said with a bored expression on his face, "No bond and to be released with no bail is ridiculous. This is a murder charge against Ms. Pierce. To release her and allow no bail would send a terrible message to the community: murder carries no consequence. In fact, we request, given the pre-meditated manner in which this woman killed her father, no bail be granted, and she be remanded to county jail until the trial."

"I'll ignore the inflammatory nature of your unproven comments for now," the Judge said, "but tone it down will you Percy. You are not in front of a jury."

"Yes, your honor," Percy said without a hint of contrition in his manner or voice.

"Defense, what's your response?"

"Judge, my client is no danger to herself or others as we will be able to prove without a shadow of doubt during the prelim. Again, we request no bail and she be released until trial based on her own recognizance."

The Judge looked at his case notes and then stated, "Bail is set at $175,000. Now let's arraign her. Mr. Neely?"

"Your honor, on behalf of my client we accept the copy of the charges and waive any reading."

"Claudette Josephine Pierce, how do you plead," the judge asked as her looked toward her.

CJ cleared her throat nervously and then replied loudly, "Not guilty, your Honor."

The judge nodded and looked down at his date book. "Mr. Neely, if your client is willing to waive time, it looks like three weeks from today would be a good date for the prelim. Will it work for you?"

"Contingent on receiving copies of the police reports by tomorrow, it should be fine, your Honor," Chris replied.

CJ was startled when the guard grabbed her arm and escorted her from the holding area. She was left in a small room near the holding area and within a few minutes Chris walked in.

"I think it went well," he said with a grin.

"But, Chris, how am I going to make bail? I don't have anywhere near the $17,500 I need."

"Don't worry about it. Becky told me when I went to pick up the apartment key someone had called and offered to pay your bail and offered collateral to cover it!"

CJ sat down abruptly on the only available chair in the room.

"What? Who did?"

"I don't know. Becky said the person said they would do it on condition it is kept anonymous. They will only reveal themselves after you are released for good. I'll find out who it is when we get further along in the process."

"I can't believe it. And I can't imagine who would do such a thing."

"Come on, CJ. Don't you get it? You are a well-respected member of this community. There are probably hundreds of people who have been helped because of your efforts at Safe House. It could be one of them wants to do this to express their appreciation. Just accept it as a perk for all your hard work."

"So now what happens?" CJ asked, as she sagged against her chair in relief.

"Let's get you out of here. Trina is waiting with a change of clothes for you. She met me at the apartment and got some stuff for you. Good thing you gave me the alarm code. So, get changed. I'll post your bail and sign you out. Then, we have work to do to get these charges dropped."

Somewhat in a daze, CJ followed his instructions. Lola brought in the clothes Trina picked up. In less than an hour, she walked out of the courthouse with Chris by her side into a delightful fall day. The fall colors and crisp air never looked and felt so good. The words, "Free,

Free at Last," reverberated through her exhausted mind as she spotted Trina standing next to her car. Injected with a sudden spurt of energy, CJ ran down the steps into her arms, ignoring the media sprinting toward her. Tears of relief sped down her cheeks as she gave Trina a big hug. The women jumped into the car and Chris yelled he would meet them at CJ's apartment.

After the incident with Sam, CJ's apartment complex put a security gate at the front and only residents and approved guests were allowed in. CJ asked Trina to stop at the gate. She could tell them to let Chris in who was in the car behind them.

Her hand shook as she tried to put the key into the lock of her apartment. Trina silently took the key from her and opened the door. As the trio stepped into the apartment, CJ stood for a minute and allowed her eyes to roam through her haven. Had it only been a day since she was so unceremoniously ripped from her normal life? It seemed like it was an eternity.

She was awakened from her musings when Chris stepped around her and put his hands on both of her arms and looked into her eyes.

"CJ, I know this is very difficult for you, but we have lots of work to do. Where do you think is the best place for us to set up for what we need to do? I don't think your apartment – lovely though it is – is going to be large enough. And my office in Chicago is too far away. Do you have some place we can use as a temporary office?"

CJ thought for a minute. "Maybe the bank will let me rent one of the vacant rooms near the Safe House office."

While CJ made a call to the bank's administrator to see if a room was available, Trina poked around in the tiny kitchen, checking to see what was available for a quick dinner. CJ told her on the way to the apartment she just couldn't face going to a restaurant to eat. So, Trina volunteered to cook.

After deciding to pick up the key to a vacant room at the bank tomorrow, CJ collapsed on to the couch and Chris sat next to her. He leaned forward, his hands on his knees and his brow furrowed in concentration as he turned toward her.

"CJ, we have our work cut out for us. Do you want to start tonight or wait until tomorrow?"

"Can we please just pretend tonight this whole thing is not hanging over my head?" CJ asked. "I would really like the chance to just relax, get to know you and spend some time with my best friend."

By now the smells of omelets were permeating the apartment and she and Chris' stomachs rumbled in unison. They both started laughing, but CJ's laughter quickly turned to hysterical tears. She was shocked at her reaction. She had always been so calm in a crisis. Chris put his arm around her and pulled her head on to his shoulder, took a white handkerchief from his back pocket, and gently handed it to CJ. Trina smiled to herself as she saw what was happening and kept right on cooking.

Chapter Thirteen

The Mystery Deepens

The informal omelet feast at CJ's apartment was just what she needed to get her mind off what happened in the last 36 hours. By unspoken consent, the trio stayed away from any discussion about accusations she killed her father. Instead, Trina and CJ encouraged Chris to talk about himself, albeit reluctantly at first. But as he relaxed over a second glass of iced tea, he skillfully entertained the women with humorous stories of some of his Legal Aid clients.

"I think probably the funniest client I had was a poor elderly woman who was accused of stealing a bunch of grapes from the fall outdoor market held weekly near the Merchandise Mart. While it is true we have a lot of unusual clients at Legal Aid, I knew I was in for quite a treat when I first saw Sophie Longhoofer at the police station. The dear lady has since passed away, so I'm not telling any stories out of school," Chris said as a disclaimer.

Trina and CJ chuckled at the woman's name.

"Yeah," Chris confirmed with a grin, "Not only was her name really Sophie Longhoofer, but she kept reminding everyone she met her name was Longhoofer, not Longhooker."

The chuckles turned to laughter as he started to describe Sophie.

"She was tall and skinny and dressed in a 30's style shapeless dress but with long sleeves and a high collar. I didn't want to stare, but it looked to me like the print in her blue dress was tiny pink frogs. On top of her frizzy gray hair she wore a blue bowler, with a large pink flower on the side. The hat was slammed down over her Dumbo-size ears, making them stick out even more. A pair of hot pink gloves and black suede pumps like what my grandmother used to wear completed her ensemble. She was neat and clean, but it was obvious she was missing a few marbles. It turned out she had Alzheimer's. She wandered almost two miles away from the apartment where she lived, escaping a careless care-giver.

"The police searched her and found her box-style purse filled with fresh grapes. Sophie was frantically trying to stuff grapes into her mouth when confronted. Long story short, the poor old girl was given a warning after I forked over the two bucks the market owner was screaming for."

The descriptions of the old woman were so vivid Trina and CJ could almost see her standing in the police station with her skinny cheeks stuffed with grapes. The humor was a great release for all three of them.

As Chris started to tell another story, CJ couldn't help but yawn. Before she could get her hand over her mouth, Chris saw it and stood up with a grin.

"Guess that's as good a signal as any it is time for me to leave," he said without a hint of unease.

CJ started to protest, but Chris put up his hand to stop her saying anything. "Really, I need to go. You've had a horrendous past couple of days and you need some rest. I'm going to be staying at my Dad's for the rest of this week, so you can either call me there or on my cell phone. What time do you want to get started in the morning?"

They agreed to meet at the newly rented office at 9 am and Chris left after thanking Trina for the dinner and reminding CJ to try and get a good night's sleep. After he left, Trina looked at CJ and said, "I thought Sam was a hunk, but Chris is even better looking; and so gentle! If I weren't already madly in love with my favorite doctor, I'd give you a run for your money, girl."

CJ blushed but her weary mind wouldn't come up with any words to refute what Trina said. Trina grinned at the rarity of no words and shooed CJ into the bedroom to take a long, hot shower and then crawl into bed.

"I'm going to clean up the kitchen while you take your shower and then I'm going to make up my bed here on the couch, like I usually do. There are advantages to being short since I can fit just right on your loveseat."

CJ was too tired to object and meekly followed Trina's instructions. By the time she crawled into bed she was operating on automatic pilot. She was asleep as soon as her head hit the pillow.

She struggled from the fog of a dreamless sleep when the phone rang at 9 am the next day. She blindly grabbed the receiver off the phone near her bed and managed a weak, "Hello."

"Good morning, CJ," Chris said cheerily. "How are you doing today?"

Without giving CJ a chance to reply, he continued with his disgustingly sunny, one-sided conversation.

"It looks like we are well on the way to getting the ridiculous charges dropped, but I don't want to get your hopes up too high yet. Detective Jasmine Dubois, the one I told you about? She will meet us at the office at 10. She's been digging and come up with some interesting information on your father."

CJ came awake with those words and could coherently confirm she would be there by 10 am. She heard Trina puttering around in the kitchen. She suddenly realized she failed to ask Trina last night how long she could stay or if she needed to get back to work. Rubbing her gritty eyes, she stumbled out of bed and quickly got dressed. Since she didn't know how much time she would be spending with Chris and how much time in her office, she put on a form-fitting, navy blue business suit, topped with a crisp white blouse. She convinced herself she was taking extra care with her appearance in case she ran into any media, not because she might spend the day with Chris. Trina poked her head into the bathroom as CJ was making the finishing touches on her hair.

"Morning, girlfriend," she said with a smile. "You are lookin' good! How are you feeling this morning?"

CJ groaned and stuck out her tongue at Trina. "Why in the world is everyone so cheerful this morning? Between you and Chris, I'm ready to puke from all the sunshine!"

Trina laughed. She was already dressed in slacks and a bright pink shirt, open at the collar. She stood in the bathroom doorway and talked as CJ finished her ablutions.

"You are the only red-head I know who can get away with wearing pink, Trina. You look great! And thanks again for your help last night. By the way, in all the excitement yesterday, I forgot to ask you how long you can stay. Don't you have to get back to work?"

Before Trina could respond, CJ gasped as she suddenly remembered Trina's wedding was just two months away. "And you have a wedding to plan," CJ said shakily.

"Don't worry about it, girlfriend. Bill and I agreed to postpone the wedding until all this stuff is over and you are declared not guilty. And, I got permission from my boss to stay here the rest of this week. I'm using some vacation time I accrued before the accident. I got a temporary leave of absence to cover the time I was in the hospital; I didn't lose any of my vacation or sick time. Besides, the boss likes me. She told me to take all the time I needed. I'm yours at least until next Monday. Let's see, today is Wednesday so it means we have five more days. We should be able to crack this case by then, don't you think?" Trina asked with a lopsided grin.

CJ was overwhelmed at the generosity of her friend. Choking back grateful tears, she hugged Trina and the two women companionably moved to the kitchen for a quick breakfast. Over the sound of cereal crunching, they agreed Trina's job would be to take care of meals and run any errands she or Chris needed. CJ realized she had to do a better job of controlling her edgy emotions if she was going to be any help to Chris and the rest of the team.

They made the short trip to the bank in Trina's car. CJ scrunched down in the back seat, just in case there were any media hanging around the apartment gate. They managed to sneak up the back steps to CJ's office without running into anyone. Becky was sitting at her desk and an expression of delight crossed her face when she saw CJ.

"Oh, CJ," Becky lamented breathlessly as she popped out from behind her desk to give her a hug, "I can't believe all of this is happening. What can I do to help? Are you okay? By the way, the new board president, Alan Larson, called to say he needed to talk to you as soon as possible."

Becky always seemed to have more energy than one person should have, despite the fact she was well past retirement age, the mother of five children and the grandmother of six. Her thin, wiry frame hid a strong constitution. Ten years ago, with CJ's help, she finally had the courage to leave a forty-year relationship with an emotionally abusive husband, who also happened to be a minister. She had been devoted to CJ ever since. CJ hired her when she took the executive director position, just after Sadie died.

CJ asked Becky to call everyone with whom she had appointments for the rest of the week and postpone them as long as she could. Becky agreed to set up a meeting with the staff for 4 pm that afternoon. "I want to explain to everyone what is going on and to assure them the work of the shelter will continue," CJ stated.

Trina headed down the hall to find Chris and see if he needed any furniture or supplies to set up CJ's legal defense headquarters while CJ called the board president. She knew Alan well, since he was a past president, so she hoped his reason for the call was to offer his help and to commiserate with her on the unfairness of the accusations. Another part of her mind, however, worried as his phone rang. Maybe he was going to fire her because of the accusation of murder; afraid the bad publicity would hurt the shelter.

She was relieved to hear him say the board was behind her and would gladly do whatever they could to support her efforts to get the charges dropped. She didn't realize she had been holding her breath until he told her of the board's support and a small explosion of air escaped as she started to speak.

"Thank you so much, Alan," CJ responded breathlessly. "I was afraid you might be going to fire me."

The CEO of the Sumter County Public Utility chuckled and then soberly said, "You need to know there are a couple of board members who wanted me to do just that. But I made it quite clear to them, everyone is innocent until proven guilty. And, as long as I am president of the board or until a court says you are guilty, you are still the shelter executive director. Besides, it would be a terrible thing for us to fire you when you have put so many years and so much effort into helping victims of injustice."

Trina poked her head into her office as CJ gratefully hung up.

"Everything okay?"

"Yes, I still have a job. At least for now," CJ said as she stood up. "How is everything with Chris? Is there anything he needs from me right now? I really have to tie up some loose ends before I can get to his office."

"Chris is a wonder-worker," Trina said with admiration. "He was able to get two desks and some chairs from the storage area of the bank at no charge! And no, I don't think he needs you right

~ 214 ~

now. He already has people from the telephone and cable companies setting up some phone and computer lines. He sent me to ask you about coffee."

After asking Becky to pick up some bagels and coffee from the Yellow Submarine, CJ got busy on some critical office work and put together an outline of what she wanted to say to the staff at the afternoon meeting. She drafted letters to the board members and major supporters, press releases for the media and everyone else she could think of to let them know the shelter was still functioning at full speed. The shelter did not have funds for a marketing staff so, like most everything else, it was added to her list of responsibilities. She sat at the computer, her fingers poised over the keyboard, as she tried to come up with the right words. By noon she completed the drafts and as she was faxing them to the board president for his approval she decided she'd better run them by Chris, too.

Drafts in hand, she walked down the hall to his temporary office. The old squeaky floor announced her arrival and Chris looked up from his laptop, smiling broadly as he saw who it was. The two borrowed mahogany desks faced the door and were arranged on either side of the narrow windows. Chris sat behind the desk on the left of the window. She wasn't sure who the other desk was for. The black, high-backed, swivel office chairs looked worn but serviceable. A dented black filing cabinet sat between the desks against the wall between the windows, easily accessible to either desk. A large banquet-style table on the left of the door sagged from the weight of three storage boxes marked on the front with the name "Reynolds." CJ figured they were the copies of the DA files. On another battered table to the right of the door were a coffee pot and a tray of bagels.

"I brought you some draft press releases and letters to donors for you to review," CJ said nervously. She wasn't exactly sure how Chris felt about her. Did he see her as just another client, a friend, or a pathetic victim?

Chris stood up and walked over to the table to refill his coffee cup.

"Come on over and have some of this great coffee," he encouraged her. "I forgot what a great cup of coffee Fred makes. You look fantastic, by the way. That is just the look we will need if we have to go to trial."

The two fell into an amicable, inane discussion of bagels, and CJ simply enjoyed the pleasure of his company for a few minutes.

"Where's Trina?" CJ asked as she sipped her coffee.

"She and Jasmine are down talking to the bank's security officer about getting copies of the tapes from the day Justin was killed."

At CJ's blank look, he reminded her Jasmine was the detective coming in this morning.

CJ took a deep breath and jumped right into the topic of payment. "While they are gone, I guess this is as good a time as any to bring up the subject of how much you charge and to see if I can somehow make arrangements for a payment plan."

"Oops," Chris said as he slapped his forehead, "I forgot to tell you. The same person who covered your bail bond is also paying all of my expenses."

CJ's mouth opened in surprise and she could feel her body relaxing now the issue was not hanging over her head.

"I am overwhelmed by this person's generosity. I don't know how I will ever be able to repay them," CJ said, struggling to keep grateful tears from spilling.

Chris reached over and touched her arm. She mentally gulped at the obvious look of compassion she could see in those expressive blue eyes of his. Just then, the noisy floor announced the arrival of Jasmine and Trina, lugging a box full of security tapes between them. Lacking any open space on the table, they sat the box down on the floor next to the table on which sat the case files.

Trina and Jasmine made an interesting contrast in appearance. Where Trina was porcelain pale, Jasmine was black as midnight. Trina was short, and Jasmine was even taller than CJ. As she observed the two, her mind conjured up the song, "Ebony and Ivory." She smiled to herself at the thought and stuck out her hand to greet Jasmine. The detective appeared to be about forty and undoubtedly still garnered a lot of attention with her knock-out figure and model-like features. Despite her height, Jasmine wore stiletto heels and was dressed in tight, black jeans and a red leather jacket over a colorful print blouse. In contrast, Trina was all frills with her curly red hair, a peasant skirt and a pink, ruffled blouse.

"Jasmine Dubois," Chris said, "This is CJ Pierce, our client."

Jasmine looked intently at CJ for a bit, sizing her up. Seemingly satisfied with what she saw, she shook her hand firmly and greeted her with a charming British accent.

"Jasmine grew up in Jamaica and went to college in London, getting a degree in crime scene investigation. We've been working together for the past five years. Believe me, you couldn't ask for a better detective on your case."

"Thank you, Jasmine, for coming all the way up here from Chicago. Do you need a place to stay while you are in town? My mother is in a rehab center right now so I'm sure you could stay at her place if you need to."

"No need," she replied. "I come from a very large family, most of who moved to the States twenty years ago. I have family all over Illinois, including an Aunt in Fredricks. I'll be fine, but thanks for the offer."

Jasmine turned to Chris and asked him if he had access to a television and a video tape deck. She would start reviewing the security tapes. CJ could tell from his expression he had forgotten to try and find one, so she quickly assured them she had one in her office frequently used for educational presentations.

With the offer, CJ realized she needed to check with the board president to get his approval to use shelter equipment for her defense. She might have to pay for its use to prevent any perception of conflict of interest, but she was confident the cost would be nominal. After confirming she wasn't needed now, CJ returned to her office until the agreed upon lunch time of 1 pm. Chris assured her he would immediately review the letters and press releases and have Trina bring them to her when he was done.

Becky ordered lunch for the defense team and joined them as they sat on folding chairs borrowed from the bank, munching on sandwiches and fruit. Trina was given the added task of keeping track of expenses. She took the lunch receipt from Becky and made a note in a small accounting book she picked up at the drug store. It was agreed meticulous notes must be kept on all expenses, not only to get reimbursed from CJ's benefactor, but also to show no shelter assets were being used for her defense.

Jasmine and Trina moved the video equipment to a nearby empty room and began looking at security tapes to see if they could spot anything unusual the day of the murder. Chris started digging through prosecution's case files while CJ and Becky tried to get a handle on the stack of shelter administrative tasks always threatening to overwhelm them. Becky dealt with the constant barrage of telephone calls from the media trying to get an interview with CJ. Alan approved the letters and press releases, with the changes Chris made, so those were sent out.

At 4 pm, CJ rode with Chris to the shelter. She made a brief statement to the staff about the allegations and assured them she was in no way connected with Justin's death, and she had no idea he was her father until the police told her. Whenever she found herself struggling through her emotions to come up with the right words, Chris was there to make calm and firm statements about the process and timeline for CJ's defense. The staff asked very few questions, seemingly satisfied by his comments. After the meeting, they surrounded CJ, hugging her and giving her loving words of encouragement and support. She was able to keep her tears locked up, thanks to Chris' calming presence.

After the staff meeting, the duo went back to the defense headquarters and picked up Trina and Jasmine for dinner at a quiet Mexican restaurant in the next town over from Fredricks, hoping the media wouldn't find them. Becky had to pick up a grandchild from daycare so was unable to join them.

They found a table in the back of the restaurant, shielded from view by a wall so they began to relax and unwind from the day's flurry of activity. As CJ silently looked around the table over steaming plates of enchiladas and tacos, she sent an arrow prayer of thanks heavenward to God for providing her with such an incredible group of people who were working on her behalf. Jasmine and Trina were getting along famously, trying to outdo each other in telling outrageous stories about people they met while working in downtown Chicago.

She was more hopeful than she had been since the arrest. She caught Chris' eye and smiled back at him as he gave her a wink as they all laughed at a story Trina just told, complete with imitations of voice and facial expressions of a fussy, obviously too rich scion of Chicago's upper crust.

Finally, at a lull in the conversation, Chris asked everyone to go home and get some rest. The preliminary hearing was only twenty days away and there was a lot of work to do.

"Do you have time to spend with me tomorrow, CJ?" he asked. "We really need to get more details on what you know about Justin and a list of every conceivable person who might want him dead."

After she assured him she would meet with him at 8 am the next day, the quartet regretfully parted company at 11 pm. Chris drove his car to the restaurant, so he dropped CJ and Trina off at the apartment and took Jasmine to her car in the bank's parking lot.

Arm in arm, CJ and Trina silently tromped up the steps to her apartment, both too exhausted from the day's events to do anything but tumble into bed.

Chapter Fourteen

The Investigation

The next day's interview with Chris was exhausting. He started the interview with prayer, asking God to give them insight and wisdom to discover who had killed Justin. He was relentless in asking CJ repeatedly if she had seen or heard anything the day Justin was killed which might help in her defense. She started the interview by giving him everything she knew about her father, including his attempt to molest her as a child and her mother's reaction to it.

"I know it looks like I had a motive to kill him," CJ said sadly, "but I really have no memory of him other than the nightmares I used to have. Besides, I had no idea Justin was my father, so why would I kill him? No one could possibly think I would kill him just because I disagreed with him as board president, could they?"

"I agree with you. So, let's look at other possibilities." He paused for a moment and then asked, "Is there any chance we could ask your mother some questions?"

"She has not been able to talk since the stroke. But we have worked out a system of question and answers which work. I ask her a series of questions and depending on her yes or no nods, I gradually am able to find out what she thinks or wants.

"She has not been told about the charges against me and I really don't know how she will react when she finds out Justin was my father."

She stopped talking for a moment as she remembered the question her mother had asked her about the picture in the newspaper of her and Justin.

"Maybe she already knows who Justin is," CJ said thoughtfully to Chris.

He looked startled at her comment. "What do you mean?"

She told him about the Taste of Fredricks fundraising event and the picture in the paper.

"She asked me who it was in the picture with me but didn't say anything more about it."

"When was her stroke?"

"I got the news right after I was released from the initial questioning by the police after the murder."

A look of horror crossed her face as she realized what Chris was asking.

"You don't think my mother could have done this, do you?"

"I don't know. But I must look at every possibility. If she recognized him in that picture as your father, it is certainly possible she snapped and decided she needed to protect you from him."

CJ could feel her heart beating so fast it felt like a drum inside her chest. Her breath began to come in short gasps as the import of what he was saying sank in. She jumped up from the chair in front of Chris' desk and started pacing around the office, her low heels beating on the wooden floor in time to her heart beats.

"No!" She said emphatically. "My mother is not capable of such a thing. And she would have told me if she recognized him."

Chris came out from behind the desk and stopped her pacing with a hand on her shoulder. "Calm down, CJ. It is only one of many possibilities. Let's not panic but think this through. Is there any way we could talk to your mother without putting her health in jeopardy? Now, come back and sit down and let's discuss how to go about this."

CJ shakily sat back down and agreed reluctantly to talk to her mother's doctor about the questions they needed to ask her, and to see if he thought she was in stable enough condition to do so. Chris continued his questions about Justin. She told him every detail she could think of about every contact she had ever had with him, including her discussion with Mr. Hawkins in Moline and her trip to the cemetery.

"I still have the picture I took of the gravestone for an infant by the name of Justin Reynolds, and the copy of the newspaper article about the courthouse fire. They are in a file at home, so I'll bring them to you tomorrow; unless you need them now?"

"I don't see any reason why this can't wait until tomorrow, CJ, but I will get Jasmine to start checking Justin's background. We can see if there is anyone who might have a motive to kill him."

While they were talking, Becky slipped into the office and quietly sat a tray on the table with some sodas and sandwiches for lunch.

"Thanks, Becky," CJ said distractedly. Becky smiled but didn't say anything and went back to her office.

As they munched on their lunch, they came up with a list of questions to ask Pam, CJ's mom, which might lead to the answers they were seeking. Just then Trina and Jasmine walked into the office, stretching and looking rather bleary-eyed.

"Oh, my God," Trina said dramatically, rolling her eyes in emphasis. "I cannot believe what an absolutely boring morning this has been! Looking at fuzzy security tapes is not my idea of a party."

Jasmine playfully punched Trina's arm. "Buck up, sweetie," she said, "We still have eight hours of tapes to go. Cheerio and all that rot!"

Chris and CJ laughed at their little drama and encouraged them to grab some lunch. They dragged four chairs together and the quartet chatted as they ate.

"Did you ladies find anything on the tapes?" Chris asked.

"Nothing yet," Jasmine replied. "But I'm trying to look for any individuals who are regulars at the bank, or anyone who doesn't fit the profile of a bank visitor. We've covered the hours before the murder and we're hoping to do the hours after the murder this afternoon. CJ, I'm going to need you to look at the tapes and see if you recognize anyone."

"Half the Village of Fredricks banks here, Jasmine," CJ lamented. "It's going to be tough to distinguish anyone who might have killed Justin. But, sure, I'll look at it and see if I see anything unusual."

Chris stood up and got a cup of coffee.

"Jasmine, CJ and I are going to visit her Mom to see if she knew Justin was her father. CJ also has a newspaper clipping and a photo I want you to check out."

He told her about CJ's suspicions about Justin and her trip to Moline earlier in the year.

"Sounds like we really need to do a thorough background check on Justin," Jasmine frowned. "Maybe there is someone in his past had it in for him. He is beginning to sound like a bit of a mystery man, and I don't like mysteries."

"This whole thing is beginning to raise more questions than answers," Chris said, shaking his head. "And we have less than three weeks before the preliminary hearing. Let's get cracking and see what we can dig up. I really want to get this case dismissed at prelim if we can."

As they finished their lunches, the group separated to continue their efforts on CJ's behalf. Chris was busy doing legal stuff so CJ went back to her office to try and get some shelter business taken care of. Trina and Jasmine went back to looking at tapes.

Later in the afternoon, CJ had to make a stop at the shelter to talk to one of the counselors who was having some problems with a client and decided to stop by her apartment to pick up the newspaper article and picture from the cemetery.

As she drove up to the apartment gate, she groaned as she saw several television trucks with reporters and cameramen lolling around. When they saw her car, they jumped into action, rushing toward her with microphones and cameras thrust forward. She decided she had better not talk to them without Chris present, so she tried to ignore the questions they were yelling at her, swiped her gate card, and sped through the gate.

She picked up the items she was looking for and called Chris to tell him about the reporters. He told her he would be at the gate in about thirty minutes and to stay in her apartment until he got there.

He called her as he pulled up to the gate. When the reporters saw CJ walking toward them, they rushed toward her. Chris got out of his car and calmly made his way through the media and stood beside CJ. "Let me do the talking, okay?" he whispered to her. CJ nodded and stood with her head up looking at Chris as he started answering questions.

"No, my client does not have anything to say at this time. Suffice it to say, CJ Pierce is innocent of these unfounded accusations, which we will be able to prove unequivocally should this matter go to trial."

Glenda Mullins, a reporter from WGN, thrust a microphone toward Chris and asked, "Why did Ms. Pierce kill her father?"

Chris had to bite his tongue to keep from saying out loud, "I just told you she didn't do it, moron."

Without hesitation, he repeated, "Ms. Pierce is innocent of the charges. Now, I know you all probably have more questions to ask, but we will not hold a press conference until after the preliminary hearing. Until then, I ask you to respect my client's right to privacy. Thank you for your time."

He put his hand on CJ's elbow and escorted her to his car. Despite the continuing barrage of questions, he didn't say anything else. They got into the car and sped off.

CJ called her mother's doctor while she was waiting for Chris and he told her he thought Pam would be fine if they wanted to ask her some questions.

"She seems to be recovering very well and even shows signs of trying to formulate words. She's able to walk with assistance so I see no reason why you and your attorney can't talk to her. Just try not to wear her out by staying too long."

CJ conveyed the information to Chris and they decided on the spur of the moment to go by the rehab center and talk to her mother.

"I think you should do most of the talking, CJ," Chris said. "She doesn't know me, and I don't want to make her uncomfortable."

As they turned a corner, down a street leading to the rehab center, Chris looked in the rear-view mirror and noticed the television van from WGN was following them.

"Uh, oh, we've got company. CJ, I'm going to try and lose them and then I'll let you out as close to the rehab center as I can get. You get out and walk to the center. Call me if you need me. I'll lead them on a merry chase while you are talking to your mother."

Tires squealed as he tromped on the gas. CJ gasped and grabbed the arm rest, letting out a little squeak of alarm as the car leaned to one side as he went around a corner. The media van wasn't quite as fast as Chris' Toyota and CJ was able to run from the car at the next block, hiding behind a delivery truck conveniently parked by the side of the road. With the van in pursuit of Chris, she nonchalantly walked back to the rehab center, just a little bit thrilled by the whole cloak and dagger escapade.

She grinned to herself at Chris' daring as she walked through the double-doors of the center. She was known to the staff so walked past the reception area to her mother's room. As she walked into the room, she was delighted to see her mother was dressed in a comfortable pair of slacks and a loose fitting, bright yellow shirt rather than the customary robe. She was seated in a large comfortable chair near the window, using her good hand to leaf through a magazine. The afternoon sun highlighted the increased silver in her hair and formed a little halo around her head. CJ swallowed the lump in her throat at how normal and pretty her mother looked, despite the obvious toll the stroke took on her. She really didn't want to disrupt this pastoral scene with some very difficult questions.

Pam looked up at CJ's entrance and smiled.

CJ pulled up a chair and sat beside her mother. "Hello, Mom. Are you doing okay today?"

Pam nodded and even managed to form her paralyzed mouth into a whispered "yeth." Surprised, CJ leaned over to hug her mother, tears threatening to fall at the effort she was exerting to talk.

"Mom, I have something I need to tell you and then I need to ask you some questions. Do you think you are up to it?

Pam looked at her quizzically, and then nodded. She proceeded to quietly tell her about the fact Justin Reynolds was her father and what led to the discovery: his death. CJ looked carefully at her mother during the telling and was surprised to see she exhibited no signs she was either shocked or dismayed at the news. Her heart began to beat faster at the possible reason why her mother wasn't reacting.

Before she could continue with the questions, she heard someone walk into the room. She turned, and her heart started beating faster as she saw it was Chris. Taking a calming breath and clearing her throat, she asked, "How did you get away from the media?"

Chris grinned and shrugged his shoulders as he told her how he simply waited beside a city bus until the van passed on the other side and then turned around and came back to the rehab center. She laughed and turned as she heard a little chuckle from her mother.

"Mom, do you remember Sadie Neely at the shelter? This is her oldest son, Chris. He's my attorney. What I haven't told you yet is the police have charged me with my father's death."

Pam's eyes widened at CJ's words and she began to tremble as she tried desperately to say something. CJ put her hand on her mother's shaking hands.

"It's okay, Mom. I didn't do it and Chris is going to help me prove it. Now I need to ask you some questions, okay?"

With an obvious effort to control herself, Pam gradually stopped shaking and looked over at Chris with a question in her eyes.

"Yes, Ms. Pierce," Chris said quietly. "We're going to prove CJ is innocent. But we need your help. Do you mind if I ask you some questions?"

Pam shook her head and looked intently at Chris.

"Did you know Justin Reynolds was your former husband?"

Pam nodded.

"Was it because you recognized him from the picture in the paper?"

Again, she nodded.

"Did you go to the bank on the day Justin was killed?"

Pam began to get agitated as she struggled to say something. CJ put her hand on her mother's arm as she leaned forward.

"Mom, we really need to know if you went to the bank on that day."

Now trembling, Pam nodded and then began gesturing. First, she pointed at herself and then made her fingers pantomime walking up some stairs.

"Okay," Chris gently encouraged her. "What happened after you walked up the stairs at the back of the bank?"

CJ was getting more and more terrified at the thought of what might be coming next. Pam continued to make her fingers walk and then pointed to her eyes as she then slumped over in the chair.

"Wait! Mom, are you saying, when you walked into the conference room you saw Justin slumped over on the table?"

Pam nodded vigorously and then made rapid walking motions with her fingers as if she was going back down the stairs.

Chris sat back and looked at Pam. "If I understand you, you are saying you saw Justin already dead in the conference room and then walked rapidly down the stairs and out the back."

Pam continued to pantomime what happened. She clutched her chest with her paralyzed hand while holding her good hand against her ear as though she was making a telephone call.

"Oh my God," CJ said in shock, "You tried to call 911 after you left, but you had your stroke and couldn't complete the call!"

Pam smiled and nodded. CJ felt such relief, knowing her mother had nothing to do with Justin's death.

"Okay, one last question, Ms. Pierce," Chris continued. "Did you see anyone else near the bank or the conference room?"

As she shook her head, Chris stood up. "Thank you so much for your help."

He turned to CJ. "We need to have you look at those security tapes and see if you can recognize anyone who entered the bank before your mother did."

They said their good-byes to Pam and headed out of the rehab center, each of them silent as they thought about what she said.

There was no sign of the media, so they made it back to the defense team's office without incident. CJ found Trina and Jasmine finishing up looking at the tapes for the day of the murder. Jasmine put the tape into the machine for the hour before the murder and CJ settled herself into a chair to watch them.

As she watched the tape CJ became more and more convinced the tapes were a dead end. She recognized most of the people on the tape. At first, she was puzzled as to why she didn't see her mother but then realized there was no security camera at the back of the bank where the steps led up to the Safe House office.

She wrote down the names of people she recognized and gave the list to Jasmine. Several of the board members entered the bank that day, as did Justin's wife, and even some of the shelter's staff members. The angle of the security camera covered the front door of the bank and the elevator which was the only other entrance to the second-floor offices. Jasmine assured her she would be talking to everyone who had entered or left the bank through the front door the hours before and after the murder.

As she finished looking at the tapes, Chris walked up and indicated he was going to need to make a quick trip to downtown Chicago on some Legal Aid business, but he would be back on the case first thing the next day. Jasmine said she was going to talk to Becky to get addresses and phone numbers for the people CJ had identified on the tape. Trina started straightening up the office and did some filing for Chris.

CJ returned to her office and tried to get some shelter business taken care of before she and Trina headed to the apartment.

Chapter Fifteen

The Prelim

The three weeks before the preliminary hearing became a blur of activity for CJ. There were the frequent team meetings and the endless questions, leaving her with a constant headache as she tried desperately to think of anything to prove her innocence and identify Justin's killer. And there were the usual barrage of administrative details and meetings associated with keeping the shelter running.

During the activity and frustrations, CJ found out who were her real friends and supporters. Every day someone would call, send her an e-mail or drop a note to let her know they were thinking about her or praying for her. But it was obvious there were other people who believed she was the killer. Their refusal to look her in the eye or carry on a conversation and the unexplained, abrupt cancellations of appointments with potential donors told her not everyone believed she was innocent. When the silent accusations threatened to overwhelm her with hurt and bewilderment, CJ would spend some time in prayer and then review an encouraging note. She kept all the positive notes in a special folder, so she could look at them when she got discouraged.

As the days went by she found her favorite times were when she could spend even a short amount of time with Chris.

He is such a caring individual, CJ thought to herself one day after a meeting with him. I wonder why he's never married. She shook off the inappropriate thoughts about her attorney and walked back into her office to attack the work in her "In" box.

Later in the day, Chris called a defense team meeting. Jasmine had returned from her trip to Moline and completed her investigation into Justin's background. As the team sat down around a make shift conference table, everyone was anxious to hear what Jasmine discovered. Without preamble, Jasmine outlined the last thirty years of Justin's life.

"Justin Reynolds was born Albert Douglass 67 years ago in Moline. He married your mother right after you were born in 1969, and they moved to Chicago, probably around 1970. By the way, CJ, have you ever looked at your birth certificate to see who is listed as your father?"

CJ look startled and then slapped her head in frustration as she realized she'd missed an important clue.

"I can't believe I never really looked at my birth certificate. Mom always had it when it was needed. I've never needed a passport and my mother went with me to get me a social security number when I started work. She handed the birth certificate to the social security worker and I never even looked at it. I think my mother still has it."

"I think you should see if you can get a hold of it," Jasmine said gently. "It might explain some things."

"I'll get it first thing tomorrow," CJ responded.

"Okay, to continue the story," Jasmine said as she tried to settle back into the hard, folding chair. "As near as I can tell, Douglass changed his name to Justin Reynolds around 1973, which fits with when you said your mother divorced him. It took some digging, but I found out he held a variety of unobtrusive jobs until 1975 when he went to college as Justin Reynolds. I got a look at his college application – don't ask me how – and there was a note saying his birth certificate burned up in a fire in the Moline courthouse. So, CJ, your instincts were right about his stealing somebody's identity.

"He graduated in 1981 with a degree in business and then for the next two decades worked as an accountant in a lot of different firms, never staying more than two or three years in one place. He's been married and divorced three times and was arrested twice for assault, but charges were dropped when the wives failed to press charges. Based on some conversations with some of his co-workers, there were rumors going around about his abusing some kids, but he was never charged. I tried to find out if any of the parents threatened him, but I got nowhere on that one.

"He married Alice Vail, his current wife, three years ago and they moved into her family home in Lake Forest. They have no children and he apparently had no children from his previous marriages. Now, here is where it gets interesting. Apparently, Alice is the only daughter of the founder and president of Vail Software, the company Justin, slash Archie, worked for. She had never been married before and was regarded as being under the thumb of her tyrant-father all her life. I haven't interviewed her yet, but she's next on my list."

There was a collective sigh of amazement from the team as they sat back in their chairs trying to absorb all they heard about CJ's father.

Chris finally broke the silence and said, "Great work, Jasmine. Okay, what do we do with this information? I haven't heard anything exonerating CJ, just a lot of red flags needing to be pursued."

He paused for a minute before continuing. "Jasmine, I want you to set up an interview with Alice Reynolds. CJ, I need for you to get a hold of your birth certificate and, by the way, I want to talk to you immediately after this. Trina, could you take Jasmine's information and put it into the computer in a timeline format, including everything we know about him since he moved to Fredricks? I know you need to get back to your office, but the prelim is set for tomorrow and I need to put all of this together. Let's all meet back here at 8 am tomorrow, and then go to the courthouse together for the prelim. In the meantime, if any of you run into anything which might be helpful for tomorrow, call me immediately."

The team stood up and moved toward their respective duties. Although Trina went back to work two weeks before, she still managed to come in one day a week to help with the defense efforts. CJ stayed behind to talk to Chris.

"CJ, I hate to tell you, but unless something happens between now and tomorrow morning, we don't have enough information on who might have killed Justin – I mean Albert – to prevent this from going to trial. By the way, let's continue to call him Justin, since it is the name by which everyone knew him."

He took a deep breath and leaned forward in his chair. "So, here is what will happen tomorrow. The purpose of the preliminary hearing is to show there is probable cause to believe a crime has been committed and you may have committed the crime."

CJ went pale and started to object, but Chris raised his hand and she stopped what she was going to say. "I know this is hard for you. I know you didn't do it. But the court doesn't care what you or I think. The court will only look at the facts and then determine if there is enough evidence for this to go to trial. The court's big issue is premeditation. And with premeditation there are three factors the prosecution must present to the court. First, is there evidence of planning on your part taking place prior to the homicide? Secondly, the prosecution must show you had a motive to kill. based on your relationship to the decedent. And, finally, the manner of the killing from which can be inferred a preconceived design."

As the reality of what was happening sank in, CJ began to tremble. Chris moved from his chair at the head of the table and sat down beside her. He took her hands and turned her to face him.

"CJ, I'm trying to get you to understand the process. If this goes to trial, it does not mean you are guilty or I'm giving up. It only means we have more time to prove you are innocent. I am going to do everything I can to prevent this from going to trial, but you need to know it will probably happen. Here's why. The fact you set up a meeting alone with Justin the prosecution will say was premeditation. The fact he was your father and he abused you suggests motive. And, finally, the means of how he was killed shows the murder was preconceived."

CJ took a deep breath and then said, "Thanks for being honest with me, Chris. I know there are explanations for everything you've said, but I also know from my experience with the court system it really does appear justice is often blind. I trust your judgment and will try very hard to maintain a modicum of dignity through this whole thing. I know I could never get through this without your help."

As she at Chris, CJ found a steadiness and strength which seemed to imbue her with confidence. She wanted to lose herself in his eyes rather than face the reality of her situation. Time seemed to stand still as they sat together holding hands.

Chris suddenly cleared his throat and stood up. He started to walk away and then turned to her and sat back down. "CJ, I promised you when we first started on this journey together I would be honest with you. So here it goes."

He looked down and his confidence suddenly changed to shyness. He took her hands again.

"I find myself starting to care for you in a way I never thought I would feel again. I was engaged about five years ago and she left me for another man. I was devastated and thought I could never love again. With you, I find hope I might be able to get past the hurt. But I also know I'm your attorney and right now I need to focus on getting you out of this mess and not on building a relationship with you – providing you feel the same way, of course," he said with a wry grin. "Besides, having a relationship with a client creates huge ethical and conflict of interest issues."

CJ's heart started the old drum beat again, but she also found deep within her a wellspring of joy threatening to engulf her in a way she never felt with anyone before. She tightened her grip on Chris' hands and smiled as she looked at him.

"Chris, I am feeling the same way. And this is a whole new feeling for me."

She told him about Sam during one of their many interviews, so he knew about the marriage fiasco.

"Just the promise of a possible future relationship with you, and with God's help, I know I can get through this horror. Thank you so much for telling me how you feel. I will keep your words locked in my heart until, hopefully, someday I'll be able to unlock them."

The two of them laughed as they realized how hokey it all sounded. Without a word, they each returned to their duties with a new understanding of their relationship and a commitment to hold it in abeyance until the time was right.

The next day's preliminary hearing went just like Chris predicted it would. Although he argued against the premeditation, the judge didn't take long for his deliberations. Trial was set for four months away. The whole thing was over in two hours.

The defense team walked out of the courtroom and faced a throng of news people. Jasmine and Trina quietly moved to the side and went to get the car. Together, Chris and CJ stood behind the microphones. He read a statement which again stated firmly CJ's innocence. He took a few questions from the media and then escorted CJ to the waiting car.

The team met at what was quickly becoming their favorite meeting spot: the Mexican restaurant.

After a relaxing lunch, they agreed to take the weekend off and meet on Monday at the office. Trina would do what she could in her spare time, using her computer at her apartment and then come in each Friday to help.

Chapter Sixteen

A Shock

Chris sat at his desk in the defense team's headquarters, his head in his hands. It was two weeks before the trial. The defense team had been working hard but was no closer to identifying a possible killer and exonerating CJ. Jasmine's interviews produced no clues. CJ could tell as she walked into the room something was bothering him. He didn't even look up when the tapping of her heels shattered the quiet of his contemplation. She walked behind the desk and gently put her hand on his shoulder. He looked up, obviously startled from the touch.

"Okay, Chris, what's going on? Something is bothering you."

Chris sat back in his chair, a pensive look on his face.

"Hi, CJ. Yeah, something is bothering me and I'm really struggling with what to do."

He paused for a minute as CJ pulled up a chair to sit beside him.

"I went back over the bank's security tapes from the day of the murder. Something has been bothering me, but it has taken me until now to figure out what it is."

He took a deep breath, looked at CJ and tightened his grip on her hands.

"CJ, the person who is paying for your legal expenses and who put up the bail money may be the murderer."

CJ was speechless as she thought about the ramifications of his statement. If the person who had anonymously stepped up to pay the costs was the murderer, what did that mean in terms of her defense? And how would they prove it if it was true? Wasn't there an issue of conflict of interest here if it were true?

Chris voiced her unspoken questions and then said, "I want you to look at the tapes again and see if you see what I do. I've also called Jasmine and asked her to join us. She should be here soon. I want to make sure I'm not the only one who sees it before I say anything."

As CJ thought about it, she realized they would have no choice: if the murderer was also the one covering her expenses she would have to figure out another way to pay the legal costs. The silence between Chris and CJ stretched as they waited for Jasmine. CJ was thinking she might go back to her Safe House office until Jasmine arrived, but then she heard the elevator and decided to wait.

"What's up, boss?" Jasmine asked as she entered the office. She pulled up a chair and sat back, putting her feet up on Chris' desk as she leaned back. Jasmine managed to make even blue jeans looked spectacular. Today she wore blue jeans tucked into black leather stiletto boots and a white oxford shirt with the sleeves rolled up. A gold chain belt topped the outfit. Large, gold hoop earrings completed the outfit.

"We need to look at the security tapes again. And this time I want the two of you to see if you can identify anyone who comes into the bank through the front door who doesn't go back out the front door. If I'm right, the murderer came in the front door and then after killing Justin, went out by the back steps."

The trio moved to the conference table where Chris already set up the television and the video tape. They arranged their chairs in front of the set and Chris pushed the "play" button. CJ grabbed a note pad and pen so she could keep track of everyone going and coming on the tape.

The time on the tape said 2 pm on the day of the board meeting and murder, just 30 minutes before the board meeting ended. As she watched the grainy video, she wrote down the names of people she recognized and put a check mark beside their names when she saw them leave.

At 2:45 she saw board members leave from the elevator. Chris slowed down the tape, so she could make sure she had identified everyone who was crowding out of the elevator after the board meeting. As she watched the last board member left the elevator, she saw Justin's wife, Alice, get into the elevator. CJ leaned closer to the television and watched carefully. No one else entered the elevator until the police arrived 30 minutes later. There was no sign of Mrs. Reynolds leaving by the elevator.

Her eyes wide in shock, CJ looked over at Chris and saw he was watching her and not the television. He nodded at her, knowing she had picked up on the same thing he had.

Jasmine let out a yell. "Bloody hell, she never came down the elevator."

"So, if I understand correctly, Chris, you are inferring Alice killed her husband and then went down the back steps of the bank? And she's the one who has been paying my legal fees? Why would she do that?" CJ asked in disbelief. "What do we do now with this information?"

Chris was quiet for a moment and then he asked, "CJ what do you want me to do? If we pursue this, it is not only possible but probable she will cut off funding for your legal defense. And, at this point, the tape is the only thing we have which circumstantially indicates she could be the killer."

Jasmine stood up and glared at Chris. "You don't seriously think CJ would give up finding the killer just to pay for her defense costs?"

Before he could reply, CJ also stood up and moved to Jasmine. She gently put her hand on her shoulder and then turned to Chris. "The two of you have no idea how much I appreciate all you have done for me. Your obvious faith in me and my innocence is incredible. But this is a decision I have to make."

She paused and then a wry grin spread across her face. "I just thought of something. I think I know what we can do."

She turned again to Jasmine. "Jasmine, can you set me up with a wire? I think it is time I paid a visit to Mrs. Reynolds."

Chris stood up so suddenly his chair fell backwards. "No way, CJ. If she is the killer, you could be putting your life in danger if you meet with her."

CJ held up her hand to stop further discussion. She then began to make her case to Chris and Jasmine.

"Here's what I think. I think Mrs. Reynolds was probably abused by Justin. She must have come to the bank to confront him and she lost it when she tried to talk to him, picked up the trophy and hit him over the head. If she is anything like the domestic violence victims I've dealt with over the years, this was a one-time, situation rage which might even be defined as self-defense. I seriously doubt she would ever hurt me. Maybe she decided to pay my legal fees to make up for what she did, hoping I would be proved innocent.

"Talking to her is really the only option we have right now. Jasmine, you didn't get anything from Mrs. Reynolds when you talked to her, right?"

Jasmine shook her head. CJ turned to Chris.

"Chris, if I wear a wire, is what she says admissible in a court of law; providing she even says anything incriminating?"

Chris thought about it for a minute. "My guess is, if we go to the police and talk to a judge, we might be able to get authorization. If we do this right, and she confesses on the tape, we could get the charges against you thrown out. I don't like putting you into a situation like this, but I don't think anyone else could get anything from her. Jasmine, if we can get over the legal hurdles, can you set it up in such a way we could get help to CJ if she is in any kind of danger?"

Jasmine nodded. She borrowed CJ's writing pad and pen and began to make a list of the things she would need to set up the wire. Chris moved to his desk and started making telephone calls to set up meetings with the police and the judge to get the necessary approval. CJ started making a list of questions she could ask Mrs. Reynolds which might lead to a confession. Her years of experience with domestic violence victims gave her an edge when it came to figuring out what might have triggered such a violent reaction from Mrs. Reynolds.

Chapter Seventeen

A Sweet Suspect

"Are you sure you want to do this, CJ?" Chris asked nervously as Jasmine checked to make sure the tiny microphone taped to CJ's bra was working. She showed CJ how to put in the earpiece and then pulled her hair over it so it wouldn't show.

CJ smiled and put her hand on his arm. "I'll be fine, Chris. We both know this is the best way to try and get a confession from Mrs. Reynolds. Besides, Jasmine and the police will be just around the corner of her house listening in the undercover van. And, in case you haven't noticed, I'm almost twice the size of Mrs. Reynolds."

She could tell Chris was still worried about her. She was deeply touched by his obvious concern and caring. There just wasn't enough room in the van for Chris so he reluctantly agreed to stay at the defense team's office.

Jasmine finished with her adjustments on the receiver and proceeded to again go through the agreed upon steps they would use in the operation. CJ would try and get Mrs. Reynolds to talk about her husband and her relationship to him and ask some pointed questions about the murder. A uniformed policeman from the Highland Park police department and Detective Tipton stood at the door of the defense team office waiting impatiently for Jasmine to complete her preparations. A judge signed the necessary papers for the wiretap and a search warrant. Detective Tipton negotiated with the Highland Park police to have an officer in on the sting, since Mrs. Reynolds home was not in the Fredricks townships jurisdiction.

"Are you sure Mrs. Reynolds is home?" she asked Chris.

He nodded. "I called her a few minutes ago and asked her a question about Justin's background, and then I asked her if she would be home for the next couple of hours in case I needed to call her. She told me she was going to be home all day. Now remember, the code words indicating you are in danger are, 'Something has to give'."

CJ dutifully repeated the words while she fidgeted with the tape from the wire causing her to want to scratch. Nothing more was said as they left the office and walked down the steps at the back of the bank. CJ turned as she started to get into her car and saw Chris waving from the top of the steps. She smiled, waved, and climbed into her car, fastening her seat belt and checking to make sure the police van was behind her as she slowly exited the parking lot.

Her stomach fluttered with a combination of nervousness and excitement, as she drove the fifteen miles to Mrs. Reynolds home located in an exclusive neighborhood near Lake Michigan. What she was about to do could free her from the nightmare of the last several weeks. At the same time, she couldn't help but feel concerned for Mrs. Reynolds. If she confessed to Justin's murder, she would end up in the same situation in which CJ now found herself: charged with murder.

It was a beautiful spring day and traffic was light at ten o'clock in the morning. In less than half an hour, CJ negotiated all the stop lights and approached the exclusive, gated community where Mrs. Reynolds lived. The team decided to not have CJ make an appointment with Mrs. Reynolds but to show up unannounced. Hopefully, she would be so surprised by CJ's visit she would tell the security guard to let her in. Jasmine would simply show the legal papers to the security guard and not indicate to which home the police van was going to not alert Mrs. Reynolds.

As she approached the security gate, CJ slowed down. The guard approached her car, and she rolled down her window, putting a big smile on her face.

"I'm here to see Mrs. Reynolds at 625 Lake Shore Drive."

"Is she expecting you?" the bored guard asked as he jotted down her license plate number.

"No, but her late husband was my father so I'm sure she'll want to see me. I'm CJ Pierce."

Evidently, he didn't associate her name with Justin's murder. The guard went back into his little house and called Mrs. Reynolds. CJ held her breath as he briefly talked on the phone. What was she going to do if she wouldn't see her? Finally, the guard hung up the phone and pushed a button to open the gate. He made no comment, other than to give CJ the directions to the Reynolds home. As she pulled through the gate, she looked in her rearview mirror and saw the police van about a block away slowly approaching the gate.

She took her time driving to the house, wanting to make sure the van made it through the gate okay. While she meandered down the road, she couldn't help admiring the view of Lake Michigan on her right and the incredible mansions on her left. She'd never been inside the exclusive complex before. Boy, would I like to have a fundraiser for Safe House at one of these houses. We could probably gain a lot of high-end donors, CJ mused.

She looked in the rear-view mirror and picked up speed as she saw the police van not too far behind her. A few blocks later, she saw the Reynolds home sitting on a rise about a hundred feet back from the road. The house number on the mail box was the only clue as to who lived in the house. Designed to look like a medieval manor, the large, dark gray stones paraded up the sides of the three-story house all the way to the gabled roof. At both ends of the house large chimney's hinted at fireplaces on each level. The house had an ancient look, softened only by the blooming azaleas and rhododendron bushes edging the driveway and surrounding the well-manicured lawn. Large, budding oak trees lined the property behind the house and on both sides of the lawn. The curtains on all windows were shut. Wow, CJ thought to herself, Dear old dad did pretty well for himself.

She shivered a bit at the foreboding feeling of the house but straightened her shoulders back as she exited her car and strode up the half-dozen steps to the large door. She stumbled a bit, startled when she heard Jasmine talking in her ear.

"Hey, love, we're not far away. We're parked a few feet away behind some bushes."

"Thanks, Jasmine," she said quietly into the microphone taped under her shirt.

Seeing no door-bell, she lifted the large gold door-knocker and let it fall with a loud bang. While she waited, she smoothed down the skirt of the pink suit she was wearing. She read somewhere pink was a soothing color. She figured it wouldn't hurt to wear it for this meeting with Mrs. Reynolds. The door was opened by a maid dressed in a traditional black and white uniform.

"Hi, my name is CJ Pierce and I would like to see Mrs. Reynolds."

"Mrs. Reynolds is expecting you, Ms. Pierce; the security guard called and said you were coming. Follow me, please."

The maid looked to be about forty years of age. She was razor-thin, with graying hair. Her face was lined and seemed to indicate life had not been easy for her. CJ couldn't help but wonder if the maid knew anything about the day of the murder. She would have to look for an opportunity to ask her some questions. This was the first time in her life she had ever been in a house with a real live maid; and one in a traditional uniform too. She couldn't help peeking around corners into various elegantly decorated rooms as they walked down a long hallway toward what looked like a sun room or sitting room at the back of the house. Wow, CJ thought to herself. The inside is much more welcoming and cheery than the outside.

"Mrs. Reynolds will be with you shortly," the maid said and abruptly left.

If I had a house like this, this would definitely be called a sun room, CJ thought as she looked curiously around the large room. The entire curved wall in front of her was made from leaded glass and looked out on a budding flower garden and an expansive yard as big as a football field. The copious trees hid views of any neighbors' homes. CJ looked up and saw the dome ceiling of the sunroom was also made of leaded glass. The room was larger than her entire apartment. All furniture was white wicker and topped with expensive looking, pale blue flowered cushions. There was enough furniture in the sunroom for three different conversational groups. Large vases of freshly cut azaleas and rhododendrons sat on every end table.

CJ was startled to hear a soft voice behind her saying, "This is my favorite room in the whole house."

Mrs. Reynolds approached her wearing a pale blue jersey dress, offsetting her beautiful, snow-white hair. A simple, single-strand pearl necklace and button pearl earrings were her only jewelry. She was probably a little over five feet tall, and she walked with an assurance CJ didn't remember from the first time she met her at the Taste of Fredricks fundraiser for Safe House. She looked like she aged a lot since CJ last saw her. It was still hard to tell her age, though, since her face was without wrinkles. She guessed she might be around sixty-five. Mrs. Reynolds shook CJ's hand firmly, but CJ couldn't help but notice a slight tremble in her hand.

"Hello, Mrs. Reynolds," CJ said. "I'm CJ Pierce. Thank you so much for agreeing to meet with me, especially on such short notice."

"Why don't we sit, Ms. Pierce?" Before she joined CJ on the nearest sofa, Mrs. Reynolds turned to the maid who was waiting in the doorway. "Sybil, will you please bring us some tea and some of those scones from breakfast?"

As the maid left the room, Mrs. Reynolds turned to CJ and said, "Now what can I do for you?"

Nervously CJ cleared her throat and found herself changing what the defense team had agreed would be the focus of the conversation: the murder of Justin Reynolds. She had questions about her father and decided she wanted to get those out of the way first.

"Mrs. Reynolds, I'm sure you know by now Justin was my father." CJ hesitated a moment and then asked, "Did you know before he was killed he was my father?"

"You do cut right to the chase, don't you," Mrs. Reynolds said with a small, tight smile.

"Justin mentioned to me the week before he died he thought you were his daughter. Up until that time I had no idea he even had a child. I knew he was married before, but he never mentioned you. I think he fully intended to ask you some questions about your mother after the board meeting the day he died."

There was a moment of silence while CJ tried to decide where next to go with the conversation. She wanted to ask what kind of person he was. Did he want to get to know her? But before she could ask any of the questions swirling in her head, Sybil walked in with a silver tea pot on a matching tray. Scones were artfully arranged on a crystal plate beside fragile tea cups and delicate napkins. She sat the tray down on the coffee table in front of the sofa and quietly left the room.

"Did you know he abused me as a child?" CJ asked abruptly after she was gone.

Mrs. Reynolds gasped in surprise and put her hand over her mouth. For a moment, CJ was afraid she might faint. Tears began to well up in her eyes and her whole body began to tremble as she looked at CJ in horror.

CJ gently put her hand on Mrs. Reynolds's arm. "It's okay, Mrs. Reynolds. I've come to terms with it. It happened when I was four years old. I really don't remember it. I had some bad nightmares for years, but those stopped after my mother only recently told me what happened. I'm sorry if I upset you, but now, while I'm trying to come to understand this whole murder thing, I decided to come and talk to you to see if you could help me figure out who might have killed him. I know I didn't kill him, but I'm afraid I may get convicted of the crime anyway since there do not seem to be any other suspects. And, the police seem to think I had motive since he abused me when I was young."

CJ stood up suddenly as she was startled to hear Jasmine speaking into her ear piece, "Get to the point, cookie."

To cover her sudden movement, CJ started pacing in front of the sofa. "Mrs. Reynolds, I need your help. My attorney told me you are the person who paid my bail and you have been covering my legal expenses."

Mrs. Reynolds started to say something in protest, but CJ held up her hand and kept talking. "I know. I wasn't supposed to know. And thank you for your generosity. But now I do know, I would really like to understand why you are being so generous. We met only the one time at the Safe House fundraiser. Why would you do such a thing for someone you don't even know; especially the person accused of murdering your husband?"

She stopped her pacing and turned to look at Mrs. Reynolds, whose hands were white from clasping them so tightly in her lap. She bowed her head and was silent for a moment before she reached up and took CJ's hand, pulling her down to sit beside her on the sofa.

"This may take a while, my dear. So why don't you sit and I'll try and explain."

She appeared to be thinking about how to start telling her story as she picked up the tea pot. CJ was silent as Mrs. Reynolds methodically poured the tea, handed a cup and a napkin to her and picked up her own tea cup. After she had taken a sip of tea, she sighed and started to talk.

"I had never been married before I met Justin four years ago. I am sure you will appreciate the irony of my situation since you work at a domestic violence shelter. My father is eighty-eight years old and he has pretty much controlled my life with an iron hand; like what I've read occurs in domestic violence situations. Although he never hit me, I guess you could say he emotionally abused me. Since it was the only life I knew, I just accepted the situation. I'm rather weak, you see," she shrugged indifferently.

"It was just easier to let Papa tell me what to do with my life. I had my books and my needlework and really didn't care much for social events.

"Over the years there were times when men showed an interest in me, but Papa always put a stop to it. My mother died giving birth to me so there was just Papa and me. He said the men were all gold diggers and really didn't love me; they only wanted his money. Four years ago, on his 84th birthday, Papa had a stroke. The employees thought Papa was still in charge since Justin would convey to them instructions he said were from Papa. Even the board thought Justin was speaking for him. Justin pretty much took over the day to day operations. Papa is now in a retirement home. He doesn't know me or anyone else for that matter. The doctor says he has Alzheimer's, on top of the damage done to his brain from the stroke."

She shook her head as CJ started to express her sympathy. "I have accepted Papa's condition. We were never close anyway. Unfortunately, Papa did not leave any instructions on what to do with the company if something happened to him. And, since I am his only child, I felt it was my responsibility to make sense of what was going on with the business. But then Justin stepped in and convinced me he would take care of everything.

"Since I really didn't know anything about the business and I didn't want to handle it anyway, it was easier just to turn everything over to Justin's control. Three years ago, he asked me to marry him. By that time, I thought I loved him."

She paused and looked down. CJ could see a hint of a blush on her cheeks.

"Justin was the first man who ever asked me to marry him. I know it sounds silly at my age, but I was like a school girl. And Justin was very good at manipulating me to get what he wanted. I believed every word he said."

She sighed. "I guess he was like my father: controlling and domineering. And it was just easier to go along with what Justin wanted rather than to think for myself; the way it was with Papa."

"The morning Justin was killed, Papa's attorney called me to say Justin just left his office. Justin told him Papa signed the company and all bank accounts over to him. He wanted the attorney to notarize a type-written statement he said Papa told him to write. He even had Papa's signature on the statement. The problem was, since the stroke, Papa has been unable to write anything, let alone sign his name. The attorney refused to notarize the statement and Justin left his office furious he wouldn't do what he wanted. The attorney then called me.

"Needless to say, I was incredibly angry. I was also deeply hurt. I had to face the fact Justin undoubtedly did not love me but simply manipulated me to take over the company and get a hold of the family fortune.

"So, there it is. That's my sordid story." Mrs. Reynolds straightened her shoulders and looked over at CJ.

"I guess we both had reasons to hate your father," she said with a sad smile. "When I heard you were accused of Justin's murder, and since it was probable you were his daughter, I decided I wanted to do something to make up for my weakness and bad choices and to help you through this horrible thing. I could not imagine you would kill him since I was sure you had no idea he was your father. Over the years I read in the newspaper about the fine work you have done with Safe House. I didn't want you to know it was me covering your expenses for fear you would refuse my help."

She picked up her tea cup and took a sip. "I guess Justin's death was the shock I needed to make me start taking responsibility for my life. I will never again allow someone else to manipulate me. So, I guess you could say his death was a blessing in disguise. For the first time in my life I am in control of my own life. I guess it is never too late to set things straight."

While Mrs. Reynolds was telling her story, CJ sipped her tea and munched on a scone. When she finished, CJ put down her tea cup, wiped her mouth with a napkin and sat quietly as she thought about where to go next with her questions.

"Ask her where she was the day Justin was murdered," CJ heard Jasmine ask in her ear piece.

"Mrs. Reynolds, did you come down to the bank the day Justin was killed?"

Mrs. Reynolds looked confused. "I don't really remember much about that day. I could have gone to the bank, but my mind seems to have gone blank when it comes to that particular day. It is odd really.

It must have been because of the shock of his death. I remember talking to the attorney, but not much else. I honestly don't know if I went to the bank."

"Okay, CJ. Wrap it up," Jasmine said quietly. "I think we have enough information to serve the search warrant."

CJ stood up and handed Mrs. Reynolds her business card she pulled out while Jasmine was talking. "Mrs. Reynolds, I really need to go. I have another appointment. But if you think of anything which might help to identify who killed my father, please give me or my attorney a call."

On impulse, she added, "And if you should ever need anything or if there is ever anything I can to do help you, please let me know."

Mrs. Reynolds stood up and shook hands with CJ after taking the card. "Thank you. I have so enjoyed our little chat, my dear. I hope you will come back again. And don't worry about the expenses for your trial. I still want to help out to make up for what I almost allowed Justin to do to Papa's business, and now for what I hear he did to you when you were a child."

Mrs. Reynolds sat back down and picked up her tea cup, seeming to forget the CJ was still there. CJ stood still for a moment and looked down on the obviously very sad and a bit confused woman. There was nothing she could say to help her. She turned to leave and saw Sybil standing in the doorway of the sunroom.

"Right this way, Miss," she said quietly and escorted CJ to the front door.

Jasmine's voice suddenly asked, "CJ. Ask the maid if she remembers if Mrs. Reynolds went out the day of the murder."

When they reached the front door, CJ turned to Sybil and asked her Jasmine's question.

The maid hung her head and said, "I'd rather not say, Miss. Mrs. Reynolds has been very good to me and my family, and I don't want to make trouble for her."

"Okay, thank you, Sybil." She handed her a business card. "If you think of anything or if you change your mind, could you please give me a call? Oh, and if Mrs. Reynolds ever needs help with anything, let me know."

"Yes, Miss," Sybil said with an old-fashioned curtsey and quietly shut the door behind CJ.

As she walked down the steps to her car, she felt a pang of guilt about what was soon going to happen at this house. Poor Mrs. Reynolds, she thought. This search warrant is going to be very hard for her. CJ said a little prayer, asking God to give Mrs. Reynolds strength.

She drove down the lane and turned right. Ahead she saw see the police van parked under a huge oak tree and hidden from the Reynolds house by a tall hedge. CJ pulled over behind the van and got out, pulling the ear piece out and wincing as she pulled the microphone tape loose under her bra. She knocked on the side of the van and Jasmine opened the door.

"Great job, CJ!" she exclaimed. "Come on in. The Highland Park police officer is in the process of calling for back-up and then they'll go in and begin the search."

"Hey, what's the matter?" she asked in alarm as CJ started to tear up. "Instead of looking pleased you may have uncovered the murderer, you look like you've lost your best friend."

CJ shrugged and plopped herself down on a hard bench in front of a bunch of electronic equipment in the van.

"I feel so sorry for Mrs. Reynolds. Justin obviously emotionally abused her; just like her father did. You heard her story. The poor woman doesn't have anybody. No children. No family. And her father is in an assisted living facility with Alzheimer's. Are you sure we have to do this? She's going to be devastated. Isn't there some other way we can find out if she killed Justin?"

"CJ, we have to have proof. If she killed him in a fit of rage – which it sounds like she might have done – there could well be some bloody clothes somewhere in the house. We need the evidence."

"I know," CJ said with a sigh. "But I don't have to like it. I'm going back to the office. I don't want to be here when the rest of the police arrive."

She exited the van and got into her car without another word. As she drove back to Fredricks, she did a lot of praying for Mrs. Reynolds. She was lethargically walking up the back steps when Becky poked her head out of the door and hollered she had an urgent phone call. CJ picked up her pace, running up the remaining steps.

"Hello," CJ said hesitantly.

"Miss Pierce?" a tremulous voice on the phone asked.

"Yes, this is CJ. What can I do for you?"

"This is Sybil, Mrs. Reynolds's maid. The police are searching the house and Mrs. Reynolds is in a terribly agitated state. I don't know who else to call. And you seemed so kind. And Mrs. Reynolds seemed to really like you. Could you please come?"

"Of course, Sybil. I'll be there as quickly as I can."

CJ hung up the phone and headed back down the stairs. "Becky," she yelled back up the stairs, "Cancel the rest of my appointments today. I have an emergency. Call me on my cell phone if you need anything."

Chapter Eighteen

The Beginning of the End

It was the beginning of the end of CJ's ordeal. The police found a grey suit covered in blood in the back of Mrs. Reynolds's closet. They would eventually be able to prove it was blood from Justin. CJ was sitting in the sunroom, holding a dazed Mrs. Reynolds's hands, when the police read her the Miranda rights.

When CJ arrived, an agitated and tearful Sybil opened the door. "Please hurry, Miss," she said. "Mrs. Reynolds is so confused, and she keeps yelling for the police to leave her house. I don't know what to do."

CJ could hear a hysterical Mrs. Reynolds in the sunroom, loudly protesting to a policeman. "This is my house. What are you doing here? Papa will not like your being here. And when Justin gets here he will throw you out!"

As CJ approached, she saw a policeman standing near the glass windows. Mrs. Reynolds was standing in front of him, trembling in rage and shaking her finger in his face. The policeman looked away from her when he saw CJ approaching and started to move toward her, undoubtedly to ask her what she was doing here. Mrs. Reynolds stopped her tirade for a moment and turned to see who the policeman was looking at. When she saw CJ, she looked confused for a minute and then started to collapse. CJ reached her before she hit the floor and gently moved with her on to the same sofa on which she and CJ had been sitting just thirty-minutes before. Mrs. Reynolds buried her head on CJ's shoulder, sobbing uncontrollably. She grabbed a napkin off the silver tea tray still sitting on the coffee table and silently handed it to the distraught woman.

"I didn't mean to do it. I didn't mean to do it," were the muffled words CJ could hear between sobs.

"Mrs. Reynolds, look at me," CJ finally said. As the tear-stained face left her shoulder and looked up at her, CJ could feel her own heart break from the terrible sadness she saw reflected on Mrs. Reynolds's face.

"I don't want you to say anything else until we can get an attorney here. Can you give me the name of your family attorney?"

A mask of confusion and bewilderment dropping over her eyes, Mrs. Reynolds seemed unable to respond. CJ turned to Sybil who was standing behind the sofa.

"I'll get it for you, Miss CJ," she said, eager to do something to help.

As she hurried off to find the attorney's information, CJ kept her arm around Mrs. Reynolds.

She looked up when she heard someone else enter the room. It was Detective Tipton.

"Hello, CJ. What are you doing here?"

"The maid called me. Mrs. Reynolds has no family to help her so she asked me if I could come. So, here I am."

Another policeman entered the sunroom behind the Detective, holding a pair of handcuffs.

"Wait!" CJ said from her seat. "Do you have to do that? She's not going anywhere. Let me talk to her for a minute, please?"

Detective Tipton thought for a moment and then shook her head at the policeman.

Mrs. Reynolds's sobs were beginning to abate. As she lifted her head from CJ's shoulder and took in everyone who was in the room, she started to tremble.

"It's okay, Mrs. Reynolds," CJ said soothingly. "I'm here with you. You need to go to the police station in Highland Park. I'll be right behind you in my car and I'll help you through the whole thing, okay?"

Mrs. Reynolds was silent for a moment and then looked up at CJ as a child might look at her mother. "Do I get to ride in a police car?" she asked in a little girl voice.

Shaken by the sudden change in Mrs. Reynolds, CJ could only respond with a nod as tears filled her eyes.

Eagerly, Mrs. Reynolds stood up and moved toward the policeman she was yelling at just a few minutes earlier. She reached over and took his hand, eagerly pulling him toward the sunroom door.

"Come on, Mr. Policeman. I want to hear the siren and see the lights. It's going to be fun!"

CJ looked over at Detective Tipton, who shook her head and then, without a word, walked out behind the duo heading for the police car.

By this time Sybil returned with the attorney's phone number. Her eyes wide in disbelief when she saw what was happening, the paper with the phone number written on it slipped from her fingers unnoticed.

CJ walked over and picked up the paper, giving a sympathetic hug to the shattered maid as she stood up. She walked back to the sofa and dug out her cell phone from her purse. Her hands shaking, she called the attorney and told him what was happening.

"I really think she needs a sedative and maybe even hospitalization," she told Attorney Long. "Her mind seems to have reverted to her childhood."

Attorney Long said he would contact Mrs. Reynolds's physician and have him meet her at the police station. CJ waved at Mrs. Reynolds who was happily playing with the police car siren. The professionals were taking over the situation, so CJ went back to her office.

When she arrived, she slowly walked up the stairs and into the defense team's office. Chris jumped up from behind the desk and rushed toward her, grabbing her and holding her in his arms like he never wanted to let her go. She let the tears fall in the safety of his arms and as he led her to a chair, kneeling in front of her and holding her hands as she told him everything since she left only a couple of hours ago. When she was finished with her story, Chris pulled her off the chair until they were both kneeling on the floor.

Tightly holding her hands, he looked deeply into her eyes and said, "I am so glad you are okay. Jasmine called in regular reports to me but when you came back and then left in such a hurry, I was worried something terrible had happened. Becky said only you got an emergency phone call from somebody at Mrs. Reynolds's house. It was hard enough staying here while all of you went off for the sting operation, but at least I knew what was going on. When you left here to go back into that situation, I realized how fearful I was something would happen to you."

"I'm fine, Chris. Thank you for your help. I'm just glad the nightmare is over. The web of lies has finally been untangled."

ABOUT THE AUTHOR

Marilyn L. Donnellan defines the modern Renaissance woman. An artist, writer, wife and mother, she also has a successful career as a nonprofit Chief Executive Officer, consultant, motivational speaker and trainer. She is the author of the science fiction series: *The Book Liberators*, and more than 60 books, guides, webinars and training modules on nonprofit management. Her fiction murder mystery, *Give 'til it Hurts,* is based on her first-hand knowledge of domestic violence. Other books include, *Two Faces of Me,* the story of her odyssey with Sophie Longhoofer, a character she often personifies in her motivational speaking. Donnellan has a BA degree in Human Resources Management and an MS degree in Administration.

The Book Liberators Series

2018 release

The Book Liberators: The White Warrior
The Book Liberators: The Slave Warrior
The Book Liberators: The Mother Warrior
The Book Liberators: The Daughter Warrior

Other Books by Donnellan

- *Give 'til it Hurts*
- *Nonprofit Management Simplified: Internal Operations,* CharityChannel Press
- *Nonprofit Management Simplified: Board and Volunteer Development,* CharityChannel Press
- *Nonprofit Management Simplified: Programs and Fundraising,* CharityChannel Press
- *Nonprofit Management Training Modules* (companions to the Nonprofit Management Simplified books) www.mldonnellan.com
- *Two Faces of Me,* Halo Publishing International
- *The Complete Guide to Church Management,* Xulon Publishing
- *Nonprofit Toolkits*
- *Nonprofit Training Modules*

Connect with Marilyn Donnellan
mldonnellanauthor@gmail. com
www. mldonnellan.com
www.amazon.com/author/mldonnellan
http://facebook. com/mldonnellan

Made in the USA
Columbia, SC
09 October 2022